COLONY DOWN

BATTLEFIELD MARS BOOK 2

DAVID ROBBINS

Severed Press

COLONY DOWN

INHUMAN ODYSSEY

CHAPTER 1

Captain Archard Rahn had been pushing the tank forever, or so it seemed, when the motion sensors in his battle suit pinged an alarm.

It was night, and a multitude of stars sparkled in the Martian heavens. It was also bitterly cold. If not for his badly battered but functional RAM 3000, Archard would have succumbed within minutes. The Red Planet's atmosphere was a lot thinner than Earth's. So much so, heat that built up during the day quickly dissipated once the sun went down. It wasn't uncommon for the temperature to plummet to minus 75 Celsius.

At the moment, though, the cold was the least of Archard's concerns. He activated his helmet display, seeking the source of the motion. Infrared didn't show a thing. There were no heat signatures anywhere within range. A new recruit might take that to mean the motion sensors were glitching. He knew better.

Archard stopped pushing the tank and turned. He ran a full spectrum sweep, but once again, nothing. Momentarily forgetting that everything he said could be heard on the tank's commlink, Archard quietly swore.

Right away, Dr. Katla Dkany asked, "Is everything all right out there?"

Archard hesitated. He refused to worry her unless he was sure. They were close, the two of them. An item, as people used to say long ago on their mother world. He wouldn't mind becoming even closer, but his personal life, to say nothing of his duty post as the head of security at one of Mars' three colonies, had been thrown into disarray by the last thing anyone ever expected to find: indigenous life.

Not that long ago, Archard had his career with the United Nations Interplanetary Corps all worked out. His plan was to stay on Mars a decade or so, then return to Earth and be in the fast lane for promotion.

Now, there was no telling what his future held. The top brass wouldn't look favorably on an officer who lost an entire colony.

"Archard?" Katla said.

"I'm here," Archard replied. "Everything is fine at the moment."

Everything had been fine at New Meridian, too, until the Martians appeared out of nowhere, or, to be precise, from up out of the ground, and wiped out the third and smallest of the colonies in a single day and night.

Now, Archard was on his way to the second largest colony, Wellsville, along with six more survivors. The others were in the tank, in reality a large rover built to military specs.

In addition to state-of-the-art electronics and armor plating, the tank incorporated a Directed Energy Weapon array on top.

Twelve hundred kilometers. That's how far it was from New Meridian to Wellsville. And since the tank's range with a full battery charge was only eight hundred, they were conserving power by having Archard push as often as possible. They were also shaving time. It took at least twelve hours of daylight to recharge the tank, a delay they couldn't afford. Not when the Martians might be after them.

Archard resumed pushing. He checked his faceplate display, but there was still no sign of life. He reminded himself that the Martians weren't like anything on Earth. They didn't have heat signatures. No heartbeats, either. That had puzzled him at first. Then he remembered that a lot of creatures on Earth didn't have hearts, either, sponges and jellyfish and the like.

The Martians reminded him more of crustaceans. He had been meaning to ask Katla if lobsters and crabs had hearts. As a physician and exobiologist, she would know.

Archard initiated a systems diagnostic on the RAM. He ran one every six hours, as a precaution. They couldn't afford a malfunction. He must be at top readiness every moment, just in case.

He went on pushing, his huge metallic feet thunking the ground with every stride. Suddenly, his motion sensors pinged again. This time, there was no doubt. His display registered a ripple of movement. Something was back there, five hundred meters or so, and closing fast.

That wasn't all. Whatever the sensors had picked up, the things were airborne.

At three hundred meters, the battle suit's night vision displayed four discreet images.

Archard had a hunch what they were. He'd encountered their kind before, in the bowels of Albor Tholus, a long-dormant volcano. He keyed his commlink. "Katla, who else is awake?"

"Just me," she answered. "I'm at the wheel. I spelled Private Everett."

Archard imagined the rest sprawled out in the tank's bay; Everett, Private Pasco, a woman named Trisna Sahir and her daughter, Behula, plus the orphan boy, Piotr Zabinski. "Wake Everett and Pasco. Tell them we have company. Hostiles. I'm going to engage."

"Wait…" Katla said.

Archard didn't dare let the Martians get close enough to the tank to damage it. Kicking in the RAM's thrusters, he went airborne himself, arcing up and away. As he flew, he magnified the images on his display. As he had suspected, the creatures were identical to the things he'd fought in the depths of the volcano.

To the scientists back on Earth, the very idea of Martians, let along the flying variety, would be preposterous. And yet there they were, each as black as the night, with eight pairs of short wings, their vitals protected by a thick carapace. A pair of forelimbs with spikes at the end were folded close to their bodies. He would have thought it aerodynamically impossible for them to fly, but they did, much like hummingbirds.

Archard arced higher to get above them. The creatures didn't react. They seemed to be focused on the tank. Bunching the RAM 3000's huge fists, he boosted his thrusters to the max, and dove. For some reason, they didn't detect his presence until he was almost on them. Then the nearest slowed and reared in his direction, and he slammed into it like a meteorite, pulverizing its underside as if it were so much mush.

The other three were instantly on him, from both sides and below. Archard punched and kicked and knocked two away, but the third thrust a spike at the RAM. He twisted to avoid it and felt the spike scrape his chest plate. Ramming the battle suit's knee into the creature's frontal ridge, he sent it spinning.

His reprieve was temporary. The other two were already converging.

Extending his right arm, Archard let them get so close he could see their multifaceted eyes glittering in the starlight. He activated his flamethrower. There was the loud whoosh of chemical fire, and both Martians became blazing balls. The pair dropped like rocks, the stubs of their charred wings beating uselessly.

The creature he had kneed did the last thing Archard expected, or wanted. It broke off and fled, no doubt to let the rest of its kind know where to find the tank.

Archard couldn't let that happen. He took off after it.

Chief Administrator Levlin Winslow's last memory was of having his head ripped off. So when he abruptly became conscious, he was considerably surprised.

His confusion was compounded by a strange green glow that filled his vision, and a feeling of being wet. He couldn't understand how he could see or feel anything with his head detached from his body.

Winslow tried to look around, but he couldn't move. He tried to blink his eyes to clear his vision and realized he didn't have eyes to blink. In fact, when he mentally reached down inside himself, he couldn't feel his body. It wasn't there.

Shock jolted him as he realized his head really had been torn off. But then, how was he aware of the green glow? And how did he account for the sensation of being wet?

Winslow's bewilderment was boundless. Nothing made sense. For that matter, his whole life had become utter chaos since New Meridian was attacked. He figured the best way to come to terms with his predicament was to relive the sequence of events that brought him to his bizarre state.

The nightmare began, Winslow recalled, when a boy by the name of Piotr Zabinski, who lived with his parents at an outlying farm, went missing. Captain Rahn had taken the U.N.I.C. security detachment to investigate. No one expected it to amount to much.

The boy had probably wandered off. But to Winslow's amazement, the next he heard from Rahn, the boy's mother and father had been torn to pieces, and Rahn and his men were in pursuit of the creatures responsible.

Winslow had prayed the captain was wrong. After all, the oldest of the colonies had been on Mars for well over a century, and in all that time, the Earthers had been left in peace.

Why did it have to happen at my colony? Winslow lamented. Why couldn't the Martians have attacked Wellsville or Bradbury?

Winslow recalled hurrying home from his office, intending to seek safety in the secret Survival Shelter under his Domicile. But the Martians were waiting. They could bore anywhere, those fiends. They had callously slain his wife and taken him captive.

Winslow experienced again his abject fright as he was whisked along seemingly endless passages until his captors reached an underground city. The spectacle of a culture so alien, of beings so unfathomable and hostile, had been almost more than he could bear.

He vividly remembered the thousands of pinkish-red worker or soldier Martians, their carapaces about a meter around. He remembered, too, the large blue kind, nine meters in length, and his impression that they were a warrior caste. Then there was the yellow Martian he'd encountered, who appeared to hold a position of authority.

Most especially, Winslow relived being brought to a high-ceilinged chamber filled with benches and bowls and odd apparatus. The walls were lined with shelves, and on many of those shelves rested the severed heads of a lot of his fellow New Meridian colonists.

Even as he'd taken all of that in, a four-meter-tall brown Martian with an umbrella-shaped carapace had approached. He'd tried to explain that he was an important government official, and that it was in the Martians' own interest not to harm him.

Hardly were the words out of his mouth when the creature ripped off his head.

And now? Winslow had no idea. If he could, he would have cried. As it was, all he could do was imagine opening the mouth he didn't have, and screaming. When he finally stopped, it was only to gird himself to scream some more.

CHAPTER 2

Dr. Katla Dkany resisted an impulse to run to the airlock and exit the tank when the RAM 3000 streaked into the night sky. She wasn't wearing her EVA suit. Without it, she wouldn't last thirty seconds.

The Robotic Armored Man-O-War was out of sight almost immediately. Katla never had understood why the military called it that when it wasn't a true robot at all.

Twisting in the driver's seat, she reached across and poked the sleeping soldier on the passenger side. "Private Everett," she said quietly, careful not to let her voice betray her anxiety. Should they lose Archard, their chances of reaching Wellsville were next to nil.

Everett snapped awake and sat up. He hailed from the hill country of Kentucky, and often impressed her with his cat-like reactions and reflexes. "What is it, ma'am?"

"Captain Rahn has gone to investigate something he picked up on his motion sensors."

Everett bent to the dash and switched on a screen. He adjusted the controls until a blip appeared, rising swiftly. "That would be the captain." He punched a button and turned a knob and a quartet of rippling images briefly registered. "Those would be the something's."

"Martians," Katla said. Although she had never seen the flying kind, Archard had told her about them.

"Those critters must have been on our trail a while," Everett remarked, tweaking the gain.

"They're intelligent beings, not animals. Animals don't live in cities."

"City. Hive. Whatever you want to call it," Everett said. "You ask me, these Martians are nothing but overgrown bugs."

"If you insist on comparing them to home-world organisms," Katla said, "they resemble crustaceans more than insects."

7

"Call them whatever you like, Doc," Everett said. "The important thing is they want us dead so we can't warn the other colonies."

"We don't know that for certain."

"I'm a hell of a good guesser."

Katla would readily admit that the Martians had displayed amazing tactical ability in their attack on New Meridian. But she still felt compelled to say, "We need to be careful not to anthropomorphize them."

"There you go again with those big words," Private Everett said, and chuckled. "Why are you making such a fuss over this, anyhow?"

"We can't afford mistakes, and to assume they think like we do is the worst one we can make."

"I'm not much interested in how they think,"

Everett said. "Only in how they die."

Katla reminded herself that the Kentuckian was a combat trooper, not a strategist.

"We should switch places in case we have to get out of here in a hurry," Everett suggested. Rising, he came around the console.

Katla didn't argue. She had only been handling the wheel so he could rest. Getting up, she moved aside. A glance at the bay showed the other trooper, Private Pasco, as well as Trisna and her little girl Behula, and the boy Piotr, fast asleep. "It's hard to believe we're all that's left of an entire colony," she remarked.

"We don't reach Wellsville, we can kiss it goodbye, too," Everett said. "And a lot more folks live there than lived at New Meridian."

Katla checked the screen. Archard's blip was growing smaller. "What is Captain Rahn doing?"

Private Everett tapped a small ripple effect. "I believe he's killed the other three and has lit out after the last flying crab or shrimp or whatever you want to call them."

"How about if we just call them Martians?" Katla said.

"Fine by me," Everett said, "so long as we make them dead."

Captain Archard Rahn was going all-out but couldn't gain on the flying Martian. The creatures were incredibly fast.

Complicating his pursuit was the fact that the only way to detect them was to use his motion sensor, and at the speed the creature was traveling, keeping a fix was difficult.

His targeting GPS told Archard that the Flyer, as he'd dubbed them, was heading northeast. Straight for Albor Tholus, the volcano that harbored their underground city.

In his mind's eye, Archard saw yet again their vast metropolis of strange structures and relived the shock he'd felt at discovering Mars was inhabited. Contrary to everything the experts claimed, indigenous life did exist. It amazed him that the best minds in the scientific communities and military echelons could have been so wrong.

Archard gave a shake of his head, and focused. He needed to stop that Flyer. He needed to stop it now.

The RAM was fitted with an army's worth of firepower; ion cannons, magnetic bombs, a flame thrower, grenades, darts, missiles and more. Each miniaturized except for the ion cannons. He selected a conventional missile, centered the crosshairs on the Flyer's rippling image, and when the crosshairs flashed to let him know targeting had been acquired, he let fly.

The missile shot from his wrist gauntlet like a bolt from a crossbow. He followed its flight on his helmet display. When it was two-thirds of the way there, the Flyer either sensed it or heard it, and flew faster. But there was no outrunning the missile. No evading it, either, although the Flyer tried zigzagging and streaking high and then dropping low, and performing aerial loop-de-loops.

The explosion was a large orange circle on the RAM's display.

Archard needed to be certain. He honed in on the debris field. Slowing, he descended as lightly as a sparrow, a remarkable feat given that the battle suit weighed over a ton.

Once his huge boots thumped down, Archard turned on his spotlight. The bright unibeam lit up everything for fifty meters in all directions. He didn't have to look far. To one side lay part of the Martian's carapace. To the other, a severed wing. The missile had done its job.

Satisfied, Archard rose into the air and made for the tank.

He didn't like leaving the others alone. They would worry. And they were vulnerable, should the Martians attack en masse.

By Archard's reckoning, they would reach Wellsville by afternoon. Their long and arduous trek would finally be over.

He could imagine the consternation their arrival would cause, especially once word spread that New Meridian had been overrun. The devastating news would be relayed to Earth, and hopefully the U.N.I.C. would send more troops and armaments before the Red Planet lived up to its name a second time.

As a soldier, Archard should be raring to take the enemy on in pitched combat and defeat them. The thing was, it could easily turn out the other way around. The Martians vastly outnumbered the Earthers. Plus, Mars was their world. The Martians were defending hearth and home, as it were, from invaders. That gave them a psychological edge. Provided, of course, their minds were anything like those of humans.

Archard harbored a suspicion they weren't. Based on what he'd seen, he suspected that Martian psychology was as grotesque as their physiology. So much so, countering it might prove impossible.

In which case, the remaining colonies were doomed.

CHAPTER 3

For Chief Administrator Levlin Winslow, the wait was endless. He was desperate for something---for *anything*---to happen. His entire world consisted of the strange green glow. His awareness extended no further. Whatever existed beyond the glow, he couldn't guess.

It didn't help that Winslow was plagued by the constant sensation of being wet. And yet, not 'wet' in a normal sense. It was as if he was submerged in a bathtub, but there was no tub, and no water.

The sensations baffled him. They were beyond the pale of his experience. He was a politician, not a scientist. Specifically, a political appointee. He'd had to kiss a lot of butt to be given the ripe plum of a colony on Mars. But that was all right. He didn't mind currying favor. Or, as his unfortunate wife liked to call it, sucking up.

The thought stirred a twinge of sadness. Gladys had been a shrew, but to her credit, she'd stood by him his whole career, even agreeing to come to Mars, which a lot of women wouldn't have done.

Affection wasn't a factor. Neither of them loved the other. Theirs was a marriage of mutual convenience. Gladys loved the trappings that came with his position, while he loved the position itself. Put more simply, she liked money and good clothes, and he liked power. To him, the purest joy in life was manipulating others to do his bidding.

Now Gladys was dead and he was---where?

Despair took root. If he could have, Winslow would have curled into a ball and cried. Gladys would have told him to buck up and take it a like a man, but what did she know? She was a woman.

Winslow tried to empty his mind and not think about his plight. He was afraid that otherwise his despair might become so great, he'd snap. He'd go stark crazy and gibber like a madman---if he had a mouth.

He started to wonder if the horrific torture would go on forever, if perhaps this was some kind of hellish afterlife, a punishment for his devious ways. But that was silly. He wasn't evil. He didn't go around hurting others for hurt's sake. Besides which, he'd never believed in that bunk.

But emptying his mind didn't help. His despair grew worse. He was on the verge of losing all reason when, without warning, there was a change.

A faint sense of movement came over him. As if the green glow were in motion. He dismissed it as a trick of his imagination. But when it persisted, a faint spark of hope was lit. The hope that, at long last, he would get to the bottom of the mystery.

Winslow was startled when the green glow began to shrink. A definite boundary appeared, a frightening dark void, almost pitch black. Bit by bit, the blackness grew. Icy fear filled him. The fear that once the green glow was gone, so, too, would he be. The blackness was devouring him. Or, rather, his consciousness.

Winslow wanted to shriek. To rave and rant against the injustice of it all. He didn't deserve this. No one did. He should be back in New Meridian, healthy and happily living the life of power and prestige he loved.

Suddenly, Winslow was jolted as if by a powerful surge of electricity. He felt himself jump and twitch and shake. The convulsions became so violent, he was afraid they would tear him apart. Then, as abruptly as they began, they stopped.

New sensations flooded in. Sensations so strong, they were dizzying. He realized he could see. His sight had been restored. But there was something wrong with his eyes. The world around him was broken into a jumble of confusing fragments.

Winslow concentrated on one of them and it acquired crystal clarity.

Raw panic set in. For there, in front of him, squatted a crab-like Martian, its grippers poised to rip and rend.

Martian dawn was breaking when Archard descended toward the tank and landed with a loud thump. When he took a couple of steps and raised an arm in greeting, the battle suit seemed sluggish. Or maybe it was him. The wear and tear was taking a toll. Since setting out, the most he'd slept was a two-hour spell a couple of days ago. He'd have collapsed from exhaustion by now except that the RAM 3000 monitored its wearer's vitals and injected stimulants and medicine as needed.

Katla's voice crackled in his earphones. "You're back! We were getting worried."

"All taken care of, sir?" Private Everett asked.

"We're good to keep going," Archard said. Moving up behind the armored rover, he placed the RAM's giant hands against the frame. "Here we go."

"Shouldn't you rest?" Katla said.

"When we reach Wellsville, I'll sleep for a week," Archard said. "Is the tank in neutral?"

"I'm at the wheel, sir," Private Everett said. "And yes, we're all set."

"Let's do this." With a grunt, Archard resumed pushing. The suit easily absorbed the strain. He settled into a familiar rhythm, moving mechanically in more ways than one.

Boulders were everywhere, and had to be avoided. Occasional rock outcroppings rose like islands. There wasn't a single speck of green anywhere. Not so much as a hint of life.

When Archard first arrived on the Red Planet, he'd been fascinated by the Martian landscape. Here he was, on a whole new world. His fascination didn't last long, though. After a while, the vistas of nothing but dirt and rocks and more rocks and more dirt lost their appeal.

Now, gazing out over the barren surface, Archard dearly missed the forests and lakes of Mother Earth. He missed trees and grass and flowers. He missed birds and butterflies. Compared to bleak Mars, Earth was heaven, pulsing with life and rich with beauty. Lord, he couldn't wait to set foot on her again.

"Captain?" Private Pasco's voice intruded on his reverie.

"What is it?" Archard said.

"I'm in the turret, sir."

Archard raised his helmet, and the young Spaniard waved at him from the MASER bubble on top of the tank. "Thank you for letting me know," he said dryly, "since that's where you're supposed to be." During the day, anyway, to serve as a lookout.

"I've been here since they woke me, sir," Pasco said, "Watching the sky for you. Or anything else."

Archard lowered his helmet and put his back, and the battle suit, into pushing faster. "If you see something, call out."

"That's just it, sir," Private Pasco said. "I think we're being followed."

Archard stopped pushing and turned. He activated every sensor in the RAM and swept every bit of ground to the far horizon. "I'm not picking up a thing."

"This is Everett, sir," the Kentuckian broke in. "I'm not picking up anything on the tank's sensors, either."

Shifting the RAM'S legs, Archard fixed his faceplate on the turret. "We can do without false alarms, Private Pasco."

"Trust me, sir. It's not nerves," Pasco said. "Twice, right before you got back, I saw something move." He pointed toward a distant outcropping. "Over there."

"Any idea what it was?"

"I only had a glimpse," Private Pasco said. "It was low to the ground, and moved fast. But to me it looked like one of those worker Martians, or whatever they are. Could be it's been following us."

"Let's hope not," Private Everett said. "Or we're royally screwed."

Archard scowled. The last thing they wanted was for the Martians to shadow them to Wellsville. It would be New Meridian all over again.

"Wait here," Archard said to those inside, and took to the air. Rising only a couple of meters, he skimmed the surface in ever widening circles. If the Martians were anywhere around, there should be tracks.

His headset crackled and Katla said, "It could be Private Pasco only imagined he saw it. Stress can play tricks on the mind."

"I saw it, Dr. Dkany," Private Pasco insisted. "I'm a trained trooper."

"Your training doesn't cover every exigency," Katla said.

"Every what?"

"Pipe down, both of you," Archard cut in. "I'm trying to concentrate out here." He didn't blame them for being testy. They'd been cooped up in the tank for over a week. As much as they'd like to get out and stretch their legs, it required donning an EVA suit and not wandering further than a stone's throw away. Hardly worth the effort, given that time was literally of the essence.

"A word if I may, sir," Private Everett said.

"I'm listening," Archard said.

"If the Martians are out there, we can't go any closer to Wellsville, can we?"

"No, Private," Archard confirmed. "We can't." They would have to break off and head elsewhere. Anywhere. So long as it was away from the second colony. Lives were at stake. A lot of lives. Specifically, one hundred and sixty-four, including a U.N.I. C. unit with seven personnel, under the command of a Major Dwight Howard.

Archard continued to search until he neared the rock outcropping Private Pasco had pointed out. Ascending a little higher, he keyed his sensors to maximum and probed the outcropping from the top of a tower-like column at its center to a ring of boulders that spread east and west from the tower's base.

Archard suddenly stopped, and hovered. His initial impression had been that the outcropping was entirely natural, just another of the countless outcroppings that dotted the Martian surface. No two were ever alike. He'd had no cause to suspect they were anything other than random geologic formations. But now, as he increased the magnification factor on his helmet display and zoomed in on the column, something wasn't right.

Archard flew closer. The column appeared to be solid rock. The boulders, too. Yet his unease persisted. Boosting magnification to its limit, he scanned the column a second time. The surface was coarse and pitted. There was no evidence it was an artificial construct.

To be sure, Archard initiated an electromagnetic scan. He went from radio to microwaves to infrared to ultraviolet. He would have done an x-ray and gamma ray sweep, too. But at ultraviolet, his helmet display lit up like a small sun going nova. The column glowed so brightly, it hurt his eyes.

Mystified, Archard tried to make sense of it. He switched the scan off to spare his eyes, and blinked to clear them. Just in time to see an opening appear at the bottom of the column.

CHAPTER 4

The opening spread a good six meters, becoming an oval-shaped door or hatch. The next instant, out scuttled an eight-legged creature a meter in circumference, with a pinkish red carapace. From the front extended a pair of appendages that ended in long, slightly serrated grippers.

From out of hidden recesses in the carapace rose a pair of multifaceted compound eyes attached to long stalks. The eyes swung in Archard's direction, and the creature rose as high at its legs allowed. Its grippers opened and closed, making clacking sounds, and the thing came at him in a rush.

Out of the hatch behind it poured more.

Archard resorted to the RAM's M537 Minigun. Able to churn out lead at a cyclic rate of five thousand rounds a minute, it chewed the first creature and those that were emerging behind it to ribbons. But more kept streaming out of the entrance.

Archard gained altitude. It wouldn't do to let the Minigun run dry, not when they might need it again. He switched to missile mode. He would blow up the column and bring it crashing down, sealing it. But as he locked on, a different type of Martian burst out and raced with amazing speed toward the tank.

The new creature was blue, and huge, five meters high and nine meters long, at least three meters of which was a segmented tail. Its forearms, if they could be called that, were as big as the battle suits.

Archard had fought one of these this before, and barely survived. They were a warrior caste, incredibly tough, astoundingly strong. Should it reach the tank, it could easily rupture the armor plating, causing decompression. Everyone inside would die.

All this ran through Archard's mind as he engaged the RAM's thrusters and sped in pursuit.

The blue warrior's eyes telescoped and turned toward him, then quickly retracted into a ridge along the front of its carapace. The creature went faster.

"Private Everett! Private Pasco!" Archard bellowed into his mic. "You have a blue Martian, closing fast!"

"Already on it, sir," Private Everett replied.

The tank was in motion. The Kentuckian had fired up the engine and was wheeling the vehicle to engage the enemy. Like the battle suit, the tank was fitted with an array of weaponry.

To Archard's consternation, the creature began to weave in an erratic pattern, as if the thing somehow knew its quarry was about to open fire.

The tank had come to a halt. The battery charge was low, and Everett was waiting for the creature to narrow the distance.

Archard preferred not to let it. He launched a missile. Almost faster than the human eye could follow, it flashed down.

At the last split-second, the creature swerved sharply, and the missile struck the ground instead. The explosion wasn't as loud as it would be on Earth. Sound didn't travel well in Mars' thin atmosphere. Dirt and stones and dust rose in a billowing cloud.

For a few anxious moments, Archard lost sight of the Martian. He zoomed over the small crater the blast had left, but there was no body.

Archard flew clear of the dust.

Seemingly unhurt, the blue warrior was bearing down on the tank.

"Leave it to me, sir," Private Everett hollered.

The tank's twin 7.62 mm machine guns opened up.

Miniature dirt geysers erupted as the slugs stitched a path toward the Martian.

Archard clearly saw the creature hit. Yet the rounds either glanced off its thick carapace or failed to penetrate to its vitals.

The blue warrior didn't slow. And now it was barely seventy-five meters from the others.

Inside the tank, Dr. Katla Dkany gasped. "What does it take to stop that thing?" A part of her, the trained exobiologist, marveled at the creature's ability to absorb punishment and keep coming. But a larger part felt rising dread.

"Pasco!" Private Everett bawled.

"On it!" the young Spaniard yelled from the DEW array on top.

Katla heard the hum of the MASER which was short for Microwave Amplification by Stimulated Emission of Radiation. In other words, it baked living organisms alive.

The blue Martian broke stride, and shook slightly.

Private Everett let out a whoop and pumped a fist in the air. "Pour it on, Pasco! We can eat Martian lobster tonight!"

The very idea revolted Katla. She supposed it shouldn't. After all, back on Earth, she had loved buttered lobster and crab. Only these were alien crustaceans, and intelligent, and eating one, to her mind, would be a hideous violation of basic ethics.

"Look! Look!" Private Pasco shouted.

The Martian had recovered and was closing again. Lowering its carapace, it became a blur.

"It's fixing to ram us!" Private Everett exclaimed.

Katla instinctively reached for the dash to brace herself. At the speed the thing was moving, and given its bulk, it might well crush the front of the tank. She heard Trisna Sahir's daughter scream.

"The MASER can't stop it!" Private Pasco bawled.

A small hand fell on Katla's shoulder and she nearly jumped. It was ten-year-old Piotr Zabinski, who had lost his mother and father to the Martians. His eyes were wide with fright. She scooped him into her arms just as Everett flicked a toggle and a sheet of fire shot from the tank.

"The flamethrower will fry that critter to a crisp!" Everett declared.

Katla had her doubts. But the creature did come to an abrupt stop, its eye stalks sliding out of its carapace to fix on the crackling tongue of flame. She wondered if it even knew what fire was.

Up in the turret, Private Pasco yipped for joy.

His elation proved premature.

If there was one thing Katla had learned about the Martians, one aspect that impressed her the most, it was their intelligence. They had developed an entire civilization. Their ruthless attack on New

Meridian had been brilliantly conducted. They were smart, these things. As smart as humans, if not smarter.

The blue Martian proved her point by darting wide to its left. It had ascertained that the flames only came from the front of the tank. The sides were unprotected.

Trisna Sahir wailed to her gods in Hindi.

Katla felt like wailing, herself. The creature was coming toward the passenger side. Her side.

Piotr's fingers dug into her, and he buried his face in her shoulder.

Heaving out of his seat, Private Everett moved toward the bay. "I'll get into an EVA suit and try to kill it."

"There is no time for that!" Trisna cried.

Katla agreed. It would take a full minute for him to don the suit, another to go out the airlock.

She looked out her window, and nearly screamed. The blue Martian had halted right outside. As if it were curious, its multifaceted eyes peered in at her. There was no hint of emotion.

Then its grippers rose and splayed against the tank's armor plating. Incredulous, Katla watched as they dug into the armor as if it were so much cardboard instead of the most impregnable synthetic known to man.

"It is going to break in!" Trisna shrieked.

CHAPTER 5

Archard held off using a weapon because the warrior was too close to the tank. Arcing high, he saw the blue warrior move around to the side. A boost to his thrusters, and he was directly above it.

Through his commlink, Archard had heard his men doing their best to stop the thing. That the blue warrior had shrugged off the MASER was incredible. It was not supposed to be possible.

Without hesitation, Archard bunched the RAM 3000's oversized fists and went into a power dive. He was taking a gamble. His RAM had taken a terrible beating during his battle in the volcano. He'd repaired the stress fractures before leaving New Meridian, but a repair was never as strong as undamaged armor. He might crack the suit open on impact. In which case, he'd be dead within moments. If the decompression didn't kill him outright, being unable to breathe would. The air on Mars was ninety-six percent carbon dioxide.

His battle suit, like the tank and the rovers and the gigantic domes that enclosed the colonies, maintained a simulated Earth atmosphere. A breach would cause the two atmospheres to collide, as it were, with catastrophic results.

His body rigid, Archard put all that from his mind and slammed into the enormous creature's broad back. It jarred him to his marrow, even with the suit's internal buffers. There was a crunch, and a powerful blow to his chest, and then he was lying on his back in the dirt and the Martian terrain and sky were swirling round and round.

Struggling to regain his senses, Archard made it to his hands and knees. The RAM's servos seemed to still be functioning. He wanted to check for leaks but that would have to wait.

The Martian wasn't dead. It lay on its side five meters away, its grippers and legs thrashing. Its carapace was cracked, but the thing didn't appear to be severely hurt.

Archard gulped a breath, and rose. Simultaneously, so did the Martian. For all of ten seconds, they stared at one another.

Archard raised a gauntlet but before he could fire, the creature came at him like a living express train. He raised his arms protectively a split moment before the Martian plowed into him with enough force to lift the RAM off its metallic feet.

The strength of the thing! Archard hit hard and slid a good four meters. He lumbered erect as the Martian rushed him with its grippers spread to seize and tear.

Archard resorted to a dart, firing when the warrior was almost on him. That close, he didn't need to rely on the suit's targeting system.

The dart struck the Martian in the equivalent of its face, and by design, instantly broke into a hundred tiny razor-sharp flechettes that sliced through the creature from its eye stalks to its segmented tail. That would be enough to kill most anything. But not the blue warrior. It slowed, and shuddered, and came on again, its will as indomitable as its body.

Grabbing both forelimbs, Archard wrenched with all the power the RAM possessed and tore one of the appendages off. Still gripping the other, he drove his fist into the carapace below the eyes, again and again and again. He struck so many times, he lost count. He punched until he felt something give and heard a squishing sound. The forelimb he was holding went limp.

Breathing deep from his exertion, Archard stepped back.

The front of the blue carapace was a ruin. Broken sections lay on the ground, and a greenish ochre dripped from the ruptures.

"Take that," Archard said, and wearily grinned.

"Captain! Captain!" Private Pasco shouted. "Behind you!"

Archard turned. He'd forgotten about the other Martians, the smaller ones. In large numbers, they were as deadly as the blue warrior. And a very large number were streaming across the plain toward them.

Chief Administrator Levlin Winslow wanted to scream but had no mouth to scream with. He saw the Martian soldier or worker or whatever it was freeze, and instinctively sought to back away. To his amazement, the creature scuttled back a few steps, and stopped.

Winslow waited for the thing to attack but it only squatted there, staring with those damnable eyes at the ends of stalks that never stayed still. What do you want? he mentally shouted. Without thinking, he reflexively thrust the hands he didn't have out at the thing as if to hold it at bay.

To his astonishment, the creature thrust both of its forelimbs at him, its grippers spread wide.

Winslow recoiled.

The crab-like Martian backed up another step.

Winslow shuddered.

The Martian shuddered.

Winslow realized he was facing a basalt wall. A wall so smooth, it was a virtual mirror.

The insight rocked him. No, no, no, he thought. It couldn't be. He imagined backing away, and the creature took a couple of steps back. He imagined blinking, and the thing's compound eyes dipped and rose. He imagined he *could* scream, imagined it with all his mental might, and a slit widened near the bottom of the creature's carapace.

Oh, God, Winslow thought. His mind reeled. He felt as if he were perched on the brink of an unfathomable precipice, and was about to plunge over. He grew dizzy, and nauseous, and was gripped by a violent seizure.

Reflected in the basalt mirror, the creature shook and trembled.

I've gone insane! Winslow thought. That was the answer. His mind had slipped into madness. Having their head ripped off would do that to anyone. But then, if his head had been separated from his body, how was he still conscious? How could he imagine something so bizarre as that reflection?

Terror seized him as he pitched into a bottomless black well. He fell and fell and fell. The next sensation he had was of a voice in his head.

"Assimilation matrix complete."

Winslow snapped alert, the words seeming to echo. But they weren't really words. They were more of a conscious impingement on his own.

"Welcome to the Unity."

Winslow became aware he could see. Like before, the world was broken into scores of fragments. He concentrated, and like before, they resolved into a single view. Under him was a basalt floor. High above, a basalt roof.

Directly in front of him towered one of the yellow Martians. Three meters tall and a meter long, it possessed two sets of three legs instead of the usual four to a side. It also had a large bowl-shaped carapace, unlike any of the other Martians he'd seen. Halfway down its carapace were a pair of long arms with grippers.

"We greet you, new brother."

What? Winslow thought.

"You are now of us. You and many of your kindred from the golden egg."

Winslow felt himself growing dizzy again.

"We could not salvage all of you. We tried, but some were irreparably harmed. They strenuously resisted being collected."

What? Winslow thought once more.

"You must calm your inner being, new brother. You are too agitated. Look at yourself. Perceive the magnificence of the gift we have bestowed."

Winslow willed his eyes to turn toward himself. He saw the same crab-like pinkish-red Martian he had seen in the basalt mirror.

"Look behind you and the full truth will dawn."

Winslow raised his eyes to behold a large chamber filled with creatures exactly like him.

"They are your brothers and sisters from the golden egg."

No! Winslow thought. Or, rather, silently shrieked.

"Yes," the alien consciousness said. *"We have made all of you as we are. As you would express it in your former stream of mentation, you are now a Martian."*

CHAPTER 6

Kicking in the RAM's thrusters, Archard rose above the tank. The counter on his helmet display informed him that two hundred and forty-seven Martians were in the onrushing swarm. He had enough missiles, darts and grenades to take out about a third. After that, he would rely on the ion cannons for as long as their charge lasted. Then it would be hand to hand, or hand to grippers. If he was overwhelmed, so be it. He would defend those in the tank with his dying breath if need be.

"Captain Rahn!" Private Pasco bellowed. "Above you!"

Thinking that Flyers were about to attack, Archard tilted his helmet skyward and raised his arms, prepared to unleash raw havoc. Only it wasn't the Martians.

A gleaming silver aircraft was descending swiftly toward them. A large saucer with a delta wing attached at the rear, it was twenty meters round and gave off a hum.

"Is that one of ours, sir?" Private Everett said.

The question jogged Archard's memory. A year or so before leaving Earth for Mars, he'd attended a briefing at which several prototypes for possible use on the Red Planet were presented. One was for the very aircraft now swooping out of the pale sky. Its operational designation, as he recalled, was the Thunderbolt.

"This is Major Dwight Howard, Wellsville U.N.I.C," a hard voice crackled over the commlink. "Captain Rahn? Is that you in the RAM?"

Archard replied in elation, "It is! I read you, sir."

"We have been monitoring your situation en route. You may stand down. We'll take care of those things for you."

"Sir!" Archard said gladly.

The Thunderbolt dropped until it was between the tank and the swarm. Hovering, it began to glow, becoming brighter by the moment. So bright, unshielded eyes would not be able to look at it.

The Martians came on in a living wave of eyes, limbs and carapaces, their grippers opening and closing in anticipation.

Archard remembered more of that briefing back on Earth. The Thunderbolt's main weapon was to be a newly developed device that emitted electromagnetic pulses. The effect was to completely disrupt any organism---and induce immediate death.

The Thunderbolt flared like a sun going nova. There was a tremendous crackling and sizzling. A spider's-web of writhing energy lines became briefly visible, spreading outward from the aircraft toward the Martians.

Archard didn't know what to expect. He thought maybe the creatures would be fried or react as if they were being electrocuted. But all they did was drop in their tracks. Every last one. No twitching. No writhing. No last bursts of savagery. They simply fell over and lay still.

"Madre de Dios!" Private Pasco exclaimed.

Private Everett whistled.

"Archard," Katla gasped. "Dear heaven. Wasn't that amazing?"

Archard went to reply but someone beat him to it.

"This is Major Howard to you in the tank. Radio silence will be maintained from this moment on unless I say otherwise. Is that understood?"

Archard answered for all of them. "Yes, sir."

"Good. We will escort you to Wellsville and provide cover the entire way."

"Thank you, sir," Archard said.

"Once we arrive, none of you are to talk to anyone. You're not to speak unless I grant permission. Is that understood?"

"Is something the matter, sir?" Archard asked, puzzled by the command.

"Didn't you hear me, Captain?" Major Howard barked. "Not another word."

As graceful as a swan in motion, the Thunderbolt rose and banked to gain altitude.

Archard opened his mouth to ask another question, then shut it. He was under orders, and he was nothing if not a good soldier. But he was troubled.

To coin a phrase from that famous playwright of long ago, Archard sensed that something was rotten on the planet Mars. And he did not like it one bit.

REVELATIONS

CHAPTER 7

Levlin Winslow didn't know how long he was in shock. He wasn't even aware his mind had shut down until he slowly became aware of sounds and movement, and by gradual degrees returned to the world of the living.

If you could call it that.

Raising his stalk eyes, Winslow gazed about the chamber at the dozens of other victims of the most ghastly fate imaginable. Many were completely still, probably numb with horror as he had been. Revulsion rippled through him, and he dearly wished he could cry.

"*You are conscious again. Good. We have much to communicate.*"

Winslow shifted on his eight legs and looked up at the towering yellow Martian. Go away, he thought. Leave me alone.

"*You are of the Unity. You will never be alone again.*"

I want to die, Winslow thought. Although he really didn't. He loved life too much. What he wanted was to be back in his own body and back in New Meridian wielding the authority and prestige that came from being important.

"*We appreciate the exchange can be traumatic. You will recover once you have been taught to embrace your sentience.*"

Exchange? Winslow thought. Sentience?

"*Yours has been transferred from the body you wore on the Blue World to a body that is part of the Unity.*"

Blue World? Winslow thought.

"*When we peer at it through our long-range viewers, your world appears blue. As do those who hail from it. Our scientists surmise it is because your world is mostly liquid.*"

God, Winslow thought, and would have laughed if he knew how.

"*The Source of All is fundamental to our beliefs.*"

Winslow's interest perked, and he straightened slightly on his eight legs. Wait, he thought. You things have a religion?

"*You disparage us. We are sentients, as you were and are. Forms are irrelevant. It is the sentience which inhabits the form that is paramount.*" The yellow Martian seemed to pause. "*As for* our relationship with and in the Source, it is intrinsic to our natures. It is why we do not kill except in extreme situations. It is why we did not merely dispose of you and your fellow Blue Worlders. It is why your heads were brought back and preserved until your sentience was transferred."

Winslow remembered all the dead colonists whose heads were missing. Now he knew why. He remembered, too, how their arms and legs had been torn off and placed next to their torsos. Why did you rip us apart and leave our bodies like you did? he mentally asked.

"We destroyed your bodies quickly to spare the sentience within from pain. The placement was done out of the respect that we of the Unity hold for all life."

A spike of anger caused Winslow to rail, I didn't want this! I didn't ask you to save me! I want my own body back! I want to be as I was!

"That is not possible," the yellow Martian said in Winslow's head, almost kindly. "You are now and forever of the Unity. Over the cycle to come, we will teach you how to alter your consciousness so that you become fully as we are."

I don't want to be as you are, Winslow forlornly thought.

"You will change your attitude once the fullness of our bliss is yours to share."

Winslow sagged in despair.

"Already you have shown remarkable aptitude. You attuned to your receptors much faster than many of the others, enabling us to interchange our consciousness streams."

You had no right, Winslow lamented.

"You came to our world. We did not come to yours. Here, all sentients are required to be of the Unity. When we learned of your colony, we absorbed it. In doing so, we learned of the other two. Plans are now in motion to absorb those, as well."

God help us, Winslow thought.

"Yes. Soon we will all be joined in the Unity of the Source."

Dr. Katla Dkany had seen a lot of beautiful sights in her time. A Norwegian fjord early in the morning. Jotunheimen National Park. The Lofoten Islands. But none were ever so beautiful as the twin golden domes of Wellsville rising in the distance. To know that sanctuary was at long last theirs brought a deep joy.

Katla sat back in her seat and smiled. Their ordeal was over. They would be taken care of, and protected. She would ask to be assigned to the Wellsville hospital and once again be able to do what she liked best: Help people.

Katla wondered how Archard was doing. She hadn't heard a peep out of him since Major Howard ordered them to maintain radio silence. Nor from either of the privates in the tank with her. She glanced over at the Kentuckian and saw his face set in hard lines. "Why do you look as if you want to punch someone?"

"Something isn't right," Private Everett said. "You heard him."

"Who? Major Howard?"

"Who else?"

"You're imagining, things."

"Am I?" Everett said. "He should have been glad to see us, glad we're alive. Did he sound glad to you?"

"Well, no," Katla admitted. She had been surprised by the officer's gruff tone. But then, military types weren't known for their gentle natures. Look at Archard. He had a tough-as-nails-exterior. Yes, he had a soft side, but he only ever showed it to her.

The boy sleeping in her lap roused and lifted his head.

"Are we there yet?" Piotr Zabinski said, and yawned.

"Soon," Katla said. She pointed at the far-off domes. Marvels of Earth science, they were composed of an alloy that was virtually indestructible. As a further safeguard, the alloy was covered by a transparent nanosheath that blocked harmful radiations. It was the nanosheaths that lent the domes their golden hue.

Piotr sat up, and grinned. "We'll be safe there, won't we, Dr. Dkany?"

"How many times must I tell you to call me Katla?" she reminded him. "And yes, we will." Out of the corner of her eye, she saw Private Everett give her a sharp glance.

Up in the turret, Private Pasco remarked, "I won't ever feel safe again until I'm back on Earth."

Katla could have kicked him. Comments like that would upset Piotr. Probably Trisna Sahir, too. Twisting around, Katla smiled at the black-haired mother and her daughter. "How are you two holding up back there? You must be happy the worst is over."

"Are you insane?" Trisna said.

Katla had forgotten how blunt the woman from India could be. "I beg your pardon?"

"What is there to be happy about?" Trisna said. "New Meridian has been overrun by those vile creatures. Over a hundred colonists, people we knew and worked with, friends and loved ones, are gone. Mars is not the uninhabited planet we were told it was. And the Martians are out to remove us from their world. There is nothing to be happy about that I can see. We are in as much danger as ever."

"Got that right, lady," Private Everett said.

"I just meant…" Katla said, and fell silent. They had a point, after all.

The worst might not be over.

The worst might be yet to come.

CHAPTER 8

Captain Archard Rahn wearily plodded into the largest of the airlocks that permitted entry into Wellsville. He waited as the outer door closed and the artificial atmosphere was cycled so the inner door could open without risk of decompression. The tank had already gone through.

Archard still didn't know what to make of Major Howard's cold treatment. The major had ordered him to go with the escort that would be waiting. When he'd made bold to suggest that given the circumstances, they should take him straight to Wellsville's Chief Administrator, Major Howard had replied that any meeting with the C.A. could wait, and to do as he was told.

As the inner lock began to open, Archard's helmet display flickered. That made the sixth time since his clash with the blue warrior at the tank. The RAM had sustained more damage. Exactly how much remained to be determined. He'd like to run a full diagnostic but that would have to wait, too.

The airlock finally spread wide, and Archard stepped out. Before him were the busy streets and building modules of the second colony, constructed to resemble those on Earth. After the destruction visited on New Meridian, it was jarring.

"Captain Rahn?" a voice said in his earpieces.

Archard looked down.

An officer and a corporal in combat uniforms, both fully armed, were staring up at him. Their Individual Combat Weapons were unslung and in their hands.

"I'm Lieutenant Burroughs," the officer introduced herself. She had dark hair that stuck out from under her helmet, and green eyes. "This is Corporal Arnold. We're to escort you to the Security Center."

"Sir," the corporal said. He was in his twenties, a huskie with broad shoulders and an easy smile.

Their friendliness alleviated a little of Archard's concern. "A pleasure to meet you," he said. "Your major had me thinking I must be in hot water."

"I wouldn't know about that, sir," Lieutenant Burroughs said.

"I should be going directly to your chief administrator," Archard said. "His name is Reubens, correct?"

"That is his name, sir, yes," Lieutenant Burroughs confirmed. "But our orders are to take you to headquarters and nowhere else."

"Don't you people know what's happened at New Meridian?" Archard said. "The colony has been overrun."

The lieutenant and the corporal glanced at one another, and Arnold said, "Sir?"

"By indigenous lifeforms," Archard elaborated. "The only survivors are myself and the five people in the tank."

"They are being escorted by Sergeant Kline," Lieutenant Burroughs said. "As for the rest of it, that's for you and the major to work out. All I know is that I'm to take you to the Security Center, and you are not allowed to talk to anyone along the way."

"Wonderful," Archard muttered.

Burroughs gave an apologetic shrug. "I'm sorry. But those are my instructions."

Archard vented his frustration with, "What in the hell is going on?"

"I'm sure I don't know," Lieutenant Burroughs said. Turning, she beckoned. "If you would be so kind as to follow me."

Archard noticed that once he passed Arnold, the corporal fell in behind them, effectively placing him under guard.

"Lieutenant, did your major prohibit you from talking to me, too?"

"No, Captain, he did not."

"Then answer me this. Am I to take it that the colonists at Wellsville have no idea New Meridian has fallen?"

"It's news to me, sir."

"To both of us, sir," Corporal Arnold chimed in.

"No broadcasts about the attack? No satellite images relayed? Nothing at all?" Archard pressed them in disbelief.

"Sir, so far as we're aware," Burroughs said, "New Meridian is perfectly fine."

"Look at his battle suit, Lieutenant," Corporal Arnold said. "It's dented and sputtering and giving off smoke. He's been in a battle, all right."

"That's not our concern, Corporal. We're to take him to headquarters and that's all."

"Yes, ma'am," Corporal Arnold said.

Archard smothered an impulse to curse a mean streak. He would save his anger for Major Howard. Then, by God, he would get to the bottom of this. Or else.

Dr. Katla Dkany fidgeted in her chair and drummed her fingers on the small table in the waiting room where she'd been brought after the tank arrived at Wellsville's U.N.I.C. headquarters.

Katla was furious. A Sergeant Kline and another trooper had escorted them there, and Kline had brought her to the room. He'd refused to answer her questions. His final comment as he shut the door was that Major Howard would arrive shortly, and her questions would be answered.

That was over half an hour ago.

Katla got up and began to pace. She was conscious of the security camera in a corner of the ceiling, and glared at it to let them know how mad she was.

She had paced for a good ten minutes when the door opened and in strode the commanding officer of the colony's United Nations Interplanetary Corp detachment.

"Dr. Dkany. I'm Major Dwight Howard."

Katla disliked him at first sight. He wasn't much over a meter and a half tall and had to be at least five kilograms overweight, most of it around his middle. He was also balding and had a florid face. In his hand, of all things, was a swagger stick.

"Have a seat," Major Howard said, gesturing at her chair with the stick.

"No apology for keeping me waiting?" Katla said.

"I assure you it couldn't be helped," Major Howard said. "We had to land the Thunderbolt and I had to report to my superiors. As it is, we're showing you the courtesy of talking to you before any of the others, including Captain Rahn."

"I'm flattered," Katla said dryly. She remained standing and folded her arms across her chest. "Who's this we?"

Moving side, Major Howard smiled and indicated the doorway with the swagger stick.

In walked a thin man of forty or so in an expensive suit. His face was familiar. Katla had seen it on occasion on newscasts involving Wellsville. "Chief Administrator Reubens?"

"In the flesh," Reubens replied. His voice was a reedy rasp that matched his physique. "Please do take a seat. We have a lot to discuss."

Reluctantly, Katla did as he wanted. But she sat rigid with her arms still crossed, and archly said, "I can't say much for your colony's hospitality. I could use a hot meal. I could use a bath. I could use a change of clothes. All of us could. Yet you had us marched in here like we're criminals or something."

"Please, my dear…" Reubens began.

It took every ounce of Katla's self-control not to leap across the table and smack him. "I'm not your *dear*. I'm a fellow professional and I'll be treated as such."

"I'm sorry, doctor. A slip of the tongue," Chief Administrator Reubens said.

"Explain to me why we're being treated this way. Explain why I saw no sign that your colony is preparing for an attack. Better yet, explain why Wellsville never responded to our emergency calls for help. Or why no one wants to know the details of what happened at New Meridian."

"Doctor, please. You really must calm down," Reubens said. "I hope I haven't made a mistake in talking to you first."

"How so?"

"I thought that you would be the most…" Reubens paused as if trying to come up with the right word, "…amenable. You are, after all, a physician and an exobiologist.

You're more intelligent than they are."

Barely able to conceal her sarcasm, Katla said, "I'm flattered you think so."

"Good. Now that you're being reasonable, we can proceed." Reubens folded his pale stick fingers on the table. "I will tell you everything you want to know."

"I can't wait," Katla said.

CHAPTER 9

Winslow roused from another bout of deep despair to regard the two creatures who were approaching. One was the towering yellow Martian, the other another of the small kind, like him.

"*Greetings. The next phase of your assimilation will now commence.*"

Winslow couldn't get over how the words formed in his head without the yellow Martian making a sound. Although that wasn't quite right. They didn't 'form.' They were inserted into his consciousness in a way that translated them as words so he could understand. Arcane science? A natural consequence of whatever they'd done to him? He didn't know and didn't care. He yearned to have his old life back, not this unending nightmare. I would rather be alone, he thought.

"*Alone is not good. Alone, you are sad. Alone, you do not partake of the joy of the Unity.*"

You talk about that a lot, Winslow thought. What is it?

"*The Unity is us,*" the yellow Martian replied, and motioned at itself and the other Martians and Winslow. "*The Unity is you.*"

I do not understand, Winslow admitted. Please leave me be, he thought.

"*You must be assimilated,*" the yellow Martian insisted. "*Your receptors must be fully attuned to the Unity so that what one sees, you can see. And so that you can better share your own flow of consciousness.*"

If you say so, Winslow thought halfheartedly.

The yellow Martian's appendage dipped toward the other Martian. "*This is Nilista. She has volunteered to help you.*"

Martians have names? Winslow thought in surprise. It had never occurred to him to ask. He was too mired in his own misery.

The towering creature's eye stalks lowered until its eyes were on a level with Winslow's. "*We do not call ourselves Martians. We do not call our planet Mars. To us, this is our Birth World. To us, we are the Unity. We also have discreet identities, as you of the*"

Blue World do. And we have gender differences. In a few respects, we are much alike, but in most we are not."

You call it Birth World because it is where you are born? Winslow thought.

The yellow Martian looked at the other one and they both quivered.

What? Winslow said.

"*Do not take offense, but you of the Blue World can be most obtuse.*"

You were laughing at me?

"*You find it strange we have a sense of humor?*"

I find everything about you and your kind strange.

"*We of the Unity are of more than one kind. We are born into many castes. You have much to learn, Blue Worlder. All of which will be imparted in the fullness of time. For now, Nilista will share what you might deem the basics.*" The yellow Martian straightened, wheeled, and departed.

Winslow fixed his multifaceted eyes on his counterpart. As near as he could tell, it was like him in every respect.

So your name is Nilista? And you are female? Can you read my mind like the banana does? Winslow figured that since they possessed a sense of humor, he might as well make a joke.

The female extended her front appendages, pointed at his grippers, spread her own, and motioned.

Winslow gathered he was to touch his grippers---he tended to think of them as hands---to hers. With a mental sigh, he complied. For a bit, nothing happened. He could feel her hard skin, if that is what it was, pressed against his. Is this supposed to do something? he asked.

Suddenly, as if a light switch had been thrown, Winslow's consciousness was enveloped by another. He experienced a pleasurable sensation of warmth.

"*Greetings. I am Nilista. You are aware of me?*"

Yes, Winslow thought. He wanted to add 'God, yes', but didn't.

"*I am to be your assimilator. Together, we will attune your receptors to the Unity. When we are done, you will be of the Unity and in the Unity, yet you will be you.*"

Will it hurt? Winslow thought.

"*Pain is not part of the process, no.*"

And I will still be me?

"*Your awareness will be your awareness, yes.*"

Nilista, I..." Winslow thought, and stopped.

"*What?*"

I don't know if I want to do this. I want to be as I was.

"*Impossible. I am sorry. But you will learn to accept and relish the new you.*"

I just don't know, Winslow thought sorrowfully.

"*Will you try? Will you bind with me? So that you might feel the fullness of the Unity?*"

For you, I guess, okay, Winslow thought. The moment he did, the feeling of warmth increased. He had a sense that he had pleased her.

"*I admire the strength you show. This cannot be easy. We will bind, and much will be made clear.*"

You keep using that word. Bind how? Winslow thought.

"*We will have sex.*"

"Before I begin, you must give your word that what I say will not go beyond these walls," Chief Administrator Reubens began. "In fact, before you will be granted permission to leave this facility, you must sign a non-disclosure agreement. Should you violate it, you will be immediately imprisoned without recourse to due process."

"What in the world?" Katla blurted.

Reubens leaned back in his chair. "You want to know what is going on, don't you?"

"Very much so," Katla said.

"I happen to think you should, at least enough to set your mind at rest. And to help you fully appreciate our position, and why we've done what we did." Chief Administrator Reubens studied her intently. "Do I have your word that this will stay strictly between us?"

Katla hesitated. She had a sense she was being manipulated. Yet, if she refused to go along, they would leave her in the dark.

"Try to understand my position," Reubens said. "The information I must impart is designated Ultra Top Secret. Which, need I point out, is far above your clearance rating. Technically, I'm violating regulations. My superiors might not be pleased."

"Why go out on a limb for me?" Katla asked.

"I consider it the lesser of two evils," Reubens said.

"If I don't, you'll go around telling everyone about New Meridian, and before we know it, we'll have discord on a wide scale."

Katla saw right through him. "You're doing this in your own self-interest."

"Not only mine personally, but Wellsville as a whole. The welfare of the colony must always come first."

"I don't like being forced to do something against my will."

Reubens shrugged. "Your choice, Doctor. But know this. Should you decline my offer, you will be held in a detention cell until the next supply ship from Earth arrives, and be sent back."

"You can't deprive me of due process," Katla bristled.

"On the contrary, under protocols established by the United Nations Interplanetary Council, I can."

"I've never heard of any such protocols."

"They were quietly promulgated at the highest levels, and just as quietly signed by the countries involved."

"By quietly you mean secretly."

Reubens smiled slyly. "What will it be? Your decision. Yes or no?"

Knowing, Katla decided, was better than not knowing. No matter the cost. "I give you my word."

"Excellent." Reubens looked over at Major Howard. "Leave us."

"Sir?"

"You heard me, Major. Be sure the door is shut. Have security turn off the camera and the recorder. And be quick about it, if you would, please."

Major Howard snapped to attention, pivoted on a heel, and briskly walked out.

"We'll have to wait a minute or two, I'm afraid," Reubens said apologetically to Katla. Twisting around, he stared up at the camera. When the green light on a small display turned red and then went dark, he nodded and turned to her again. "Now then. Where to begin? I would imagine you have a host of questions."

"Ten or twenty," Katla said. "Why didn't you send help to New Meridian? Why didn't Wellsville and Bradbury respond to our emergency calls? I happen to have been at Captain Rahn's side when he sent out six or seven distress signals, and I know he sent out more. Not one was answered."

Reubens shook his head. "No, that's not where we should begin. To make this easier, we should go back in time to before the arrival of the first colonists." He bent toward her. "You see, my…" he was apparently going to say 'dear' again but caught himself, "we have always known Mars is inhabited."

CHAPTER 10

Dr. Katla Dkany was so shocked, the most intelligent response she could make was, "What?"

"We have always known. By 'we,' I mean a small cadre of higher dignitaries at the United Nations as well as certain leaders of a few of the larger countries. Plus various scientists involved in projects related to the colonization."

"All along?" Katla said.

"Since the early NASA days of rover exploration," Reubens clarified. "Those feeds were carefully controlled. We never let anything slip through that we didn't want the public to know."

"Back up," Katla said. "Are you telling me that rovers were sent down into the Martians' underground cities?"

"Hardly," Reubens said, and chuckled. "We would have lost contact. But the rovers did occasionally catch images of Martians outside of caves or where have you. Not many, but enough that it was long suspected a flourishing population of indigenous life existed."

"And none of the powers that be thought it was important enough to tell the people?"

"It was the discovery of the century. Of the millennium. Hell, the most important discovery ever."

"Then *why*?"

"Think, Doctor," Reubens said. "What would have happened if NASA announced to the world that our next-door-neighbor was inhabited?"

"Celebrations in the streets?" Katla said.

"Possibly. Or perhaps condemnation. Our space program, after all, was geared toward putting colonists on Mars as soon as we were able. Imagine the hue and cry if the public had found out about the Martians. It would have been the Native American situation of early America all over again. There would have been protests. Widespread civil unrest. Riots, perhaps."

"You're exaggerating."

"Am I?" Reubens said. "You know very well that at the very least there would have been U.S. congressional investigations. Intelligence probes by different governments. Our Mars program would have ground to a halt while the court of public opinion debated the ethics of colonizing a planet that was already occupied."

"The governments and the corporations involved couldn't let that happen," Katla guessed. "Not after all the money they'd invested."

"Really, Doctor?" Reubens said. "You do our leaders a great disservice by reducing it to dollars and cents."

Katla sneered in scorn. "Are you trying to tell me they kept it a secret to protect the Martians?"

"It wasn't a matter of protecting but learning all we could. Initially, we didn't know the extent of the situation. We honestly had no conception of how developed they are."

"Initially?" Katla repeated.

"Well, of course, once Bradbury was established, we secretly sent special ops teams to gather more intel. That was when we learned the truth."

"And kept that secret, too."

"Why this obsession with our secrecy?"

"Because it was wrong."

"From your point of view. Not from ours. We had every reason to believe that if the colonists kept to themselves and didn't disturb the Martians, the Martians would leave us alone. It was why we instituted emergency protocols that would only be put into effect in a worst-case scenario."

Katla jabbed a finger at him. "You son of a bitch."

"I beg your pardon?"

"Was one of those protocols a communications blackout?"

Reubens looked down at his hands.

"It was! You bastards had a plan in place to impose a communications blackout on any colony that encountered the Martians."

"I never said that."

"You didn't have to. It explains what happened at New Meridian. Why we couldn't get through for help. Our signals were being jammed."

"Don't take it personally," Reubens said.

"And you expect me to keep silent about this?"Katla said in amazement.

"Either that," Reubens said coldly, "or we clap you in irons and return you to Earth and let them deal with you as they see fit."

"What do you think they'll do to me?" Katla said. "The truth, if you don't mind."

Chief Administrator Reubens slowly ran a finger across his throat.

The minutes turned into half an hour and then an hour and the hour into two and still no one came.

Archard simmered. He resented how he was being treated. It baffled him that no one in authority seemed to be the least bit alarmed by or interested in the debacle at New Meridian.

He had tilted his chair back against the wall so that it leaned on two legs and was sitting with his arms folded when the door opened and in walked Lieutenant Burroughs.

"Captain," she said cordially.

Archard lowered the chair and was about to rise and demand to know why he was being ignored when another person came in behind her. He was expecting Major Howard or possibly Wellsville's Chief Administrator, Evander Reubens, whom he had met once. But it was someone else, a small civilian in his forties or so, wearing a rumpled suit. His hair was in need of combing and he hadn't shaved in days. He also wore old-fashioned glasses, which was unusual given that implants had long become the norm. The man was carrying a portable holographic unit which he set on the table.

"Captain Rahn," the man said, smiling. "Don't get up on my account. We need to talk, urgently." He pulled out the other chair.

"So urgent it took two hours for you to get here?" Archard said.

The man blinked in surprise. "That long? My apologies." He offered his hand. "I'm Kylo Carter, by the way. Named after a character in some old movie." He smiled when Archard shook.

"You might have heard of me. I'm the planetary scientist."

It was Archard's turn to be surprised. The planetary scientist was the top brain on Mars, the head of all scientific endeavors. "Aren't you stationed at Bradbury?"

Carter nodded. "I am. But given the exceptional circumstances, I deemed it prudent to come here and take an active part."

"In what?" Archard asked. Only then did he notice that Lieutenant Burroughs had assumed a parade-rest stance by the door.

"I'll get to that in a moment," Carter said, pushing his glasses up on his nose. "Again, my apologies for your being neglected. I happen to know that Chief Administrator Reubens has been busy debriefing your associate from New Meridian, Dr. Dkany. And Major Howard has been dealing with a problem that we hope doesn't turn into a crisis of the first magnitude."

"What sort of problem?"

"I'll get to that in a moment, too." Carter opened the holo case and turned the unit on. "You need to be brought up to speed. Since you're in the military, you're bound by U.N.I.C. regulations not to reveal what I'm about to disclose. To forestall your many questions, permit me to answer them in advance."

Archard found himself liking this odd little man. Carter cut right to the chase, a trait Archard admired. "Are you a mind reader, too?"

The planetary scientist chuckled. "Let's put it to the test, shall we? To begin with, we've been aware that Mars has indigenous life since before the first colony was established..."

"What?" Archard exclaimed in shock.

"...and the administrative and military branches back on Earth decided it was wise not to let that become common knowledge..."

"What?" Archard said again.

"....so a policy of containment was implemented whereby should a colony make contact with the Martians, a communications blackout would be imposed..."

"Son of a bitch!" Archard started to rise but sat back down again.

"That is why, sadly, you were left on your own at New Meridian," Carter said. "It wasn't my doing. Or, for that matter,

Chief Administrator Reubens' or even Governor Blanchard's at Bradbury. They were simply following a policy I don't necessarily agree with. As a scientist, I would much rather have contacted the Martians directly long ago."

"Dear God," Archard said quietly. He was thinking of all the dead colonists at New Meridian. "They abandoned us. Left us to die."

"I understand how you must feel. I would feel the same were I in your boots. But you must overcome any emotional issues you might have and do your best to assist me. When I said this is urgent, I meant it."

Archard contained his anger enough to ask, "Urgent how?"

"Just like at New Meridian and Bradbury, Wellsville has a number of outlying farms. Agripodists who supply much needed produce."

"Yes. So?" Archard remembered that at New Meridian, the Zabinski farm had been the first place the Martians struck.

"At my suggestion, Chief Administrator Reubens had the Communication Center radio word to each of the local farm families to report to the colony under the medical pretext of being given a required booster shot."

"And?" Archard said when Carter didn't go on.

The planetary scientist pushed on his glasses again, and frowned. "Not one of them has answered."

CHAPTER 11

To Levlin Winslow, the very idea of copulating with a Martian---he couldn't bring himself to even think the other word---was loathsome. I am an Earthman, he thought, hoping he could explain to the creature that called herself Nilista without angering her. I am what you call a Blue Worlder. We do not become...... intimate.....with alien crustaceans.

"*You are one of us now*," Nilista inserted into his head. "*You are....what did you just call us? A crustacean yourself.*"

Don't remind me, Winslow bitterly thought, adding, It doesn't change anything.

"*To the contrary*," Nilista responded. "*It changes everything. You will never be as you were. You are no longer of the Blue World. You are of the Unity. Embrace the gift we have bestowed. Open your sentience to the fullness we offer.*"

To do what you want, I would have to be sick, Winslow thought.

"*Blue Worlders only have sex when they are ill? Is that how you cure yourselves?*"

No, no, Winslow thought, and mentally laughed at the absurdity of it all.

"*Then when do you bind?*"

All the time, Winslow admitted.

Nilista moved closer, her multifaceted eyes almost touching his. "*If that is so, why balk at binding with me?*"

It goes against everything I believe, everything I have ever been taught. To bind with you would be like binding with an animal.

"*I do not comprehend. Elucidate, if you would.*"

An animal. A lower lifeform. Do you have them here as we do on my world?

Nilista's eye stalks rose up and down as if she were studying him. "*You are confused. I am not a lower lifeform. You are. Or you were, before we made you one of us. Now you are of the Unity.*"

That still wouldn't make it right, Winslow thought.

"*Right how?*"

You know. Acceptable.

"*You refuse to bind with me because you find it aesthetically displeasing?*"

On a whole lot of levels, Winslow thought. He was afraid to come right out with the fact that he regarded her as hideous, and any binding as repulsive in the extreme.

"*I think I perceive the truth of it,*" Nilista said. "*You regard your previous form as the standard by which you judge all forms.*"

Of course, Winslow thought.

"*You must learn to be more accepting. Forms are fluid. Look at your own. The form your now possess is not the form you once were.*"

Stop reminding me, Winslow thought, and went on with, The important thing is that I don't want to bind.

"*I am sorry.*"

Not wanting to offend her and make an enemy, Winslow thought, You have no need to apologize. It is me, not you.

"*No. I am sorry because you have no choice.*"

Excuse me?

"*For us, binding is a biological imperative. The same as ingesting sustenance. We do it because we have to.*"

Now I'm the one who doesn't comprehend, Winslow thought. You can't force someone to bind, as you call it, against their will.

Without any forewarning of what she was about to do, Nilista raised her carapace onto her rear pair of legs with her other legs and her grippers spread wide.

What are you doing? Winslow demanded.

"*Releasing my pheromones.*"

What good will that do? It's not as if… Winslow began, and got no further. Suddenly, his mind seemed to freeze up. He was aware of his surroundings but couldn't form a cohesive thought. Then, to his utter horror, his Martian body moved of its own accord.

Toward Nilista.

The Thunderbolt hangar wasn't under the domes. The aircraft was too large to fit through any of the airlocks so it was housed in a separate structure linked to the south dome, or Dome Two, by a short enclosed walkway.

Archard was surprised that neither the walkway nor the hangar were constructed of the same nigh-indestructible alloy as the domes. Nor were they covered by the protective nanosheath that made the domes gleam like gold in ambient light.

Planetary Scientist Kylo Carter must have noticed the look of puzzlement on Archard's face because he commented, "The Thunderbolt was brought to Mars in pieces and assembled only a short while ago. There hasn't been time to build a proper facility. We will once the current situation stabilizes."

"I would admire your optimism," Archard said, "if I hadn't been at New Meridian."

"Which is exactly why I've asked you to tag along on our check of the agrifarms. You know what to look for. We don't."

"Evidence of the Martians, you mean?" Archard said.

"Exactly."

"The fact you've lost contact with the farmers is enough. The Martians are doing the same thing they did at New Meridian. First, they attacked the outlying farms, then the colony."

"We need to be absolutely certain," Carter said.

"I already am."

A metal door permitted entry into the hanger. Archard was amazed that an airlock, which would be an added safeguard against accidental or intentional decompression and was required by regulations, hadn't been installed. Nor were there any EVA suits hanging on the wall. He pointed that out.

Carter gestured at the Thunderbolt, which sat on an elevated pad. "Our suits, should we need them, or in the aircraft. As for the lack of an airlock, we saved time and money by installing an air cycling system that feeds in air from the dome and expels it as required. Besides," and he pointed again, at an open airlock on the rear of the Thunderbolt itself, "the aircraft is our haven in case of an emergency."

Archard still didn't like it. Heightened risk for expediency's sake was never wise, in his opinion.

"Shall we?" Carter said, and led the way into the airlock. They had to wait for it to cycle to enter the aircraft.

Archard had imagined an interior design as futuristic and imposing as the exterior. But no. The cockpit and the passenger seating were similar to those in a conventional craft. The big difference was the large housing for the propulsion system.

In the pilot seat, a stocky, balding man with bronze clusters on his lapels was going through a preflight checklist. A trooper with sergeant's chevrons on his sleeves was wiping the viewscreen.

"I believe you've already met Major Howard," Carter said, nodding at the officer.

"We haven't been formally introduced, no," Archard said.

"This other trooper is Sergeant Kline. Gentlemen, Captain Archard Rahn."

The pair stopped what they were doing, and turned.

Archard nodded at the noncom, then snapped to attention and gave the major a salute. "Sir."

"Mr. Carter has filled you in?" Major Howard said.

"Yes, sir," Archard replied. The man's tone was exactly the same as it had been over the radio when the Thunderbolt came to the tank's rescue.

"Good. Then we can get underway. We're making a sweep of the farms to find out why they've all gone silent."

"It should be obvious, sir," Archard said. "The Martians are on the move."

"Or it could be a communications glitch. Sunspot activity, maybe," Major Howard said.

Wishful thinking, Archard almost said.

"We'll know soon enough," Kylo Carter interjected. "If it is the Martians, we'll have time to warn the colony and prepare an adequate defense."

Archard doubted it. The attack on New Meridian had been unbelievably swift. He couldn't help but think that he was about to witness history repeat itself.

INTERLUDE IN MARTIAN MINOR

CHAPTER 12

To Dr. Katla Dkany, it smacked of the unreal to walk the streets of Wellsville and see the colonists going about their daily routines as if all was well. Ignorance was indeed bliss. They were oblivious to the fact that the Red Planet harbored creatures every bit as intelligent as they were, and that those creatures resented their presence and would wipe them out if they could.

Katla would dearly love to talk to Archard, but Chief Administrator Reubens assured her that was quite impossible for the time being.

"Captain Rahn is involved in a security matter," was all Reubens would tell her.

A private named Heinlein had ushered her from the Security Center. As he held the exit door, she'd asked if he knew where she might find Private Everett and Private Pasco. They should be able to get word to Archard, she reasoned.

Private Heinlein had smiled politely and said he had no idea where the pair were.

Now, Katla watched people chatting and laughing and behaving as if they didn't have a care in the world, and prayed it would stay that way.

Taking the vouchers Reubens had given her from her pocket, Katla examined them. She was entitled to a room at the Visitor Center, free of charge, until further notice. She was also entitled to free meals. It was the least the government could do, given that she'd lost everything except for the clothes on her back. Perhaps to partly mollify her, Reubens had also given her a credit slip useable at any store in the colony.

His generosity didn't do a thing to improve Katla's mood. She was furious that those in authority had allowed the assault on New Meridian to take place. They might argue it wasn't their fault, that the Martians had left the colonies alone for well over a century, and how were they to know the creatures would suddenly rise up in violent wrath? A lame excuse, if ever there was one.

Thinking about it made Katla so mad, she clenched her fists and swore. Coming to a stop, she willed herself to calm down. It wouldn't do any good to lose her temper, especially since she had no one to vent it on.

"Dr. Dkany? They let you go, too?"

Katla glanced up. Not three meters away stood Trisna Sahir, her daughter Behula in her arms. Beside them, holding Trisna's other hand, was Piotr Zabinski, his eyes brimming with tears.

"Katla!" the boy shouted, and threw himself at her. Wrapping his arms around her legs, he pressed his face against her and gave a little sob.

"Piotr?" Katla said, putting her hand on his head.

"He has hardly stopped crying since we were separated," Trisna said. "I tried to comfort him but all he does is say your name over and over."

"Oh, Piotr," Katla said softly. She sought to pry him loose but he clung to her as if for dear life. "Why wasn't he turned over to Social Services?"

"I do not know. The woman who spoke to us at the Security Center, an assistant to Chief Administrator Reubens, would only say that the government will look after us in due course."

"What does that mean?"

"Again, I do not know," Trisna said. "Her name was Hinds. She told us that the C.A. desires to speak with us in person, but he is too busy at the moment. In the meantime, she gave me a voucher for the Visitor Center."

Katla stroked Piotr's hair and he sniffled. "They gave me vouchers, too."

"Why do they treat us this way?" Trisna said. She didn't wait for Katla to reply. "I tried to tell them about New Meridian. About the horrors I saw. About the people who died. But this Hinds woman said they would take my official report later. It is most strange."

Katla gazed up at the high arch of the dome and then out across the streets and buildings designed to simulate those on Earth. "What counts is we don't need to worry about the Martians."

"Do you really and truly believe that?" Trisna anxiously asked.

"No," Katla admitted. "I don't."

When Archard had enlisted in the United Nations Interplanetary Corps, he'd had a decision to make. Should he join the Air Wing or the Infantry? He loved to fly. From the time he was twelve until he was seventeen, he'd spent every spare minute on his hoverboard. But he chose the Infantry.

Mars was the reason. Above all else, Archard craved to be assigned to a colony. Each had a contingent of U.N.I.C. troopers, and nearly all were Infantry. There wasn't a need for Air Wing personnel because the colonies didn't have aircraft.

Until now.

The Thunderbolt hummed like a swarm of bees as it skimmed the Martian surface far in excess of the speed it could attain on the world where it was manufactured. The thin atmosphere---less than one percent of that on Earth---and the fact that the surface gravity on Mars was considerably weaker---less than forty percent of Earth gravity---enabled the craft to outperform expectations.

The EDM propulsion system had a lot to do with it. Back at the Academy, every recruit was taught that the conventional aircraft of yesteryear wouldn't have flown well on Mars because there wasn't enough lift---that thin atmosphere again---for their wings. Helicopters were more practical, but their rotors had to be a lot thicker and spin a lot faster than on Earth. The Thunderbolt didn't rely on wings, per se, or rotors. The Delta wing at the rear of the craft wasn't for lift so much as maneuverability.

Archard stared out the horseshoe-shaped viewport that gave the crew a one hundred and eighty-degree line-of-sight on the Martian terrain. Close to Wellsville, the land was mostly flat, with occasional small hills and rock outcroppings.

Major Dwight Howard might be a hardnose, but he could fly. They were so low, Howard constantly had to avoid rock domes and spires and other obstacles, and did so with the finesse of an experienced pilot.

Archard turned to the planetary scientist, who was strapped into a seat to his right. "Why are we hugging the ground this way?"

Kylo Carter was gazing out the viewport with a huge smile on his face. He was like a kid in an old-fashioned candy store, drinking in the sights of the Red Planet. "The lower we are, the better our sensors are at picking up the Martians."

"Good luck with that," Archard said dryly.

Carter tore his gaze from the viewport. "You're referring to the fact that the Martians don't have heat signatures and sometimes barely register on our motion sensors?"

"They're next to invisible. It's why we couldn't combat them effectively at New Meridian."

Settling back, Carter adopted the air of a professor imparting information to a student. "As you must have guessed by now, the Martians are crustaceans. Like their counterparts on Earth, they're cold-blooded invertebrates. Their exoskeletons are a lot thicker than crustaceans on Earth. Which accounts for why they don't have a heat signature."

"How do you know their exoskeletons are thicker?" Archard asked.

"From the specimen our scientists examined."

Archard's surprise must have shown.

"Only a few months after Bradbury was established, those in charge took a great risk. They needed to know more about the Martians, so a special ops team went out and brought back a dead one. A particularly large blue specimen."

"A warrior," Archard said.

"Is that so?" Carter said. "You think their bioforms are function-specific? I've suspected as much. We'll have to discuss that more later." He paused. "Where was I? Oh, yes. Their anatomy. They have a simple circulatory system. For a heart, they have a sac that is largely muscle. It's located just below their upper carapace, at about the midpoint of their body."

"Good to know," Archard said. Now he knew where to aim.

"We've established that they don't have ears, as we do. Their exoskeletons are covered with microscopic hairs which enable them to pick up vibrations in the air. Given how thin the air is, and that it doesn't conduct sound well, the hairs must be incredibly sensitive."

"It would have been nice to have been informed of all this before they attacked New Meridian."

Carter ignored Archard's comment. "The surgical team conducting the examination also found several organs they couldn't explain. One was an adjunct to their brain. Another was part of their nervous system. They speculated that…"

Just then Major Howard called out, "Heads up, people! The first farm is dead ahead."

Sergeant Kline, who hadn't spoken a word the entire flight, bent toward the viewport and blurted out, "Dear God, no."

CHAPTER 13

The effects of explosive decompression were an ugly sight. With the atmosphere essentially a vacuum, any breach in a dwelling or a vehicle or an EVA suit resulted in catastrophe and death.

The farm looked as if a rampaging giant had stomped it in savage abandon. Half the house module lay in fragments, scattered over an acre. A work shed was standing but had a jagged hole in the side. The agripod itself, through which the farmers descended to their underground fields, was a buckled ruin.

"Set us down and I'll search for survivors, sir," Sergeant Kline said.

"No," Major Howard replied. "Our orders are to make a sweep of all the farms and return to Wellsville as quickly as possible."

"But the farmers, sir," Sergeant Kline said. "The families."

"I'll send a rover out after we get back," Major Howard said. Already he was banking the Thunderbolt to proceed to the next farm.

"There could be people alive down there," Sergeant Kline protested.

Kline reminded Archard of his own sergeant, McNee, who was one of the first casualties in the blossoming war.

"Enough," Major Howard said.

Kline rose even more in Archard's estimation by saying, "We're not even to search for survivors? Who would give such an order, sir?"

"That would be me," Kylo Carter said. "You heard the major. A tank will be sent out. For now, it's imperative we ascertain the extent of the Martian activity."

"Once they start," Archard mentioned, "they don't stop for anything."

"There you go," Carter said to Kline. He turned his head to stare at the receding farm. "I was hoping the agripods were all right. That we were dealing with nothing worse than a communications issue."

"I believe they call that wishful thinking."

"You are so sure of yourself," the planetary scientist said.

Archard had held back long enough. "You don't seem to be paying attention. Or is it that you only hear what you want to hear? New Meridian is *gone*. All the colonists except for the few I brought with me, are *dead*. And the same thing is going to happen to Wellsville if you don't get your head out of your ass."

"That will be enough, Captain," Major Howard said.

"Let him speak," Carter said. "In his eyes, I probably have this coming."

"In anyone's eyes who has a shred of common sense," Archard said.

"Let me hear your assessment, then. All of it."

Archard complied. "The only reason the colonies have lasted as long as they have is sheer dumb luck. The Martians didn't know we were here. They're not surface dwellers, like us. They live underground. Their cities, their tunnels, everything, is down deep. They rarely come to the surface. When they do, it's usually out of a volcano or a cave."

Archard was warming to his topic, and as he did, his anger rose, too. "Isn't it interesting that neither Bradbury nor Wellsville are located anywhere near volcanoes or caves? Almost as if it was planned that way to reduce the risk of contact?"

"A prudent precaution, wouldn't you say?" Carter said.

"What, were you experts thinking that if you could put off contact long enough, there would be enough of us here that we could hold our own if the Martians proved hostile?"

Carter scowled.

"Then came the third colony," Archard continued. "Which, strangely, isn't all that far from a volcano. Was that deliberate? Did our leaders finally want contact made? Were we the bait to lure the Martians out?"

"You're putting the wrong spin on things," Carter said. "We never suspected they would be so unremittingly hostile. Our hope was to establish peaceful relations. Can you fault us for that?"

"I can fault you for not warning the colonists," Archard said. "We had a right to know what we were getting into."

"How many from Earth would have come if they knew?" Carter said. "How many would volunteer for duty on another planet if the planet's inhabitants might not want them there?"

"A lot of people are dead because of your scheming."

Their argument might have escalated had Major Howard not called out, "The next farm is straight ahead. Looks to be just like the first."

"Not quite," Sergeant Kline said. "Some Martians are still there."

Levlin Winslow tasted euphoria, and loved it. He couldn't begin to describe the sheer ecstasy, the rapturous pleasure, he experienced. All he knew was that for as long as it lasted, every particle of his being, or his sentience, as the Martians called it, was vibrant with exquisite bliss. A bliss so potent, so intoxicating, that even as he came down out of the clouds of pure delight, he wished he could waft up into them again and stay there forever.

Gradually, Winslow once more became aware of his surroundings. Of the cavernous chamber. Of other creatures. Of Nilista, standing in front of him.

"*Have you oriented? We have learned that the first time can be unsettling to your kind.*"

I... Winslow began, and was at a loss how to explain his feelings.

"*Our binding has joined us. You to me and me to you.*"

Are you my wife?

Nilista didn't respond to the question. Instead, she said, "*Do you have a heightened sense of me now?*"

Winslow was about to say that he didn't know what that meant when suddenly he did. A flood of new sensations poured through him. It was as if he were in Nilista's head, or in her sentience, feeling the things she felt and sharing her thoughts as she thought them. What have you done to me? he asked.

"*It is a consequence of the binding,*" Nilista explained. "*Your consciousness and my consciousness are now one when we want them to be.*"

We can turn it on and off?

"To share yourself is a freewill choice. It is not constant unless you want it to be."

Conflicting emotions tore at Winslow. Unease that his inner person had been violated. Joy at his new twofold awareness.

"Open yourself further."

I don't know how.

"Think it and it will be," Nilista said.

Again, it seemed to happen spontaneously. Winslow experienced not just him and her, but as if a switch had been thrown, a deluge of new perceptions filled every fiber of his being. A hundred---a thousand---sentiences flowed side-by-side with his and hers in some sort of stream of awareness where each was separate yet part of the whole.

"You are in the Unity and the Unity is in you," Nilista said. *"You are one of us in all that you are."*

There were so many impressions, flashing at him so fast, that Winslow's mind reeled. Too much! he thought. How do I turn it off?

"You simply think it off."

Straining his will, Winslow succeeded. Suddenly, it was him and her again. And then it was just his own sentience, and no other. I did it! he thought. I'm back to being me.

"Experiment," Nilista said. *"Join with the Unity when and as you desire. Feel the others there with you. Soon you will come to know what they know, to see what they see."*

It's like nothing I ever imagined, Winslow thought.

"Other Blue Worlders are doing as you are. They have been converted, and are now one of us."

It's wondrous, Winslow gushed. I almost wish everyone from Earth could feel as I do right now.

"They can. Those who have come to our world will be converted first." Nilista gently touched her gripper to his. *"We are about to collect those of your kind in the golden eggs you call Wellsville. We will bring their heads here and do to them as we did to you."*

They will resist, just as we did, Winslow predicted.

"We are massing enough of us that the gathering should go well."

Winslow gestured at the other new converts in the chamber. What about those of us from New Meridian?

"*You will be on the front lines*," Nilista revealed. "*Helping with the harvest.*"

CHAPTER 14

Archard straightened in his seat for a better view of the second farm.

The destruction was worse. Every module lay in pieces. The agribubble had been flattened and broken apart. Usually, a short flight of stairs led underground. But the stairs appeared to have been obliterated, too, leaving a dark hole. And out of the hole were scrambling the meter-round pinkish Martians. At least a score seemed to be examining the debris.

Major Howard circled, his hand hovering over the armament controls. "Should I fry them, Mr. Carter?"

"I want to see what they're doing," the planetary scientist said.

"Gloating, maybe," Sergeant Kline said.

For some time now, Archard had been wondering if the Martians felt emotions similar to humans. Or were they biological machines, their functions dictated by their nervous systems? For that matter, did they even have nervous systems? He was about to ask Carter if the autopsy done on the warrior had revealed anything along those lines when he saw two of the creatures below drag a man-sized body by the arms from the ruins of the house module.

"That must be the farmer," Major Howard said.

"He wasn't wearing an EVA suit when his house exploded."

"What do they intend to do with him?" Carter wondered.

"Eat him, maybe?" Sergeant Kline said.

Archard hadn't ever considered that prospect. He'd seen no evidence that the Martians devoured anyone at New Meridian.

"They're taking it down into the hole," Major Howard said.

"Perhaps back to where they came from to examine it," Carter said.

"Look!" Sergeant Kline exclaimed, and pointed.

One of the Martians had seen them. Its eye stalks stopped swaying and pointed toward the Thunderbolt. The next moment, every last creature trained their compound eyes on the aircraft.

"How do they do that?" Major Howard said.

"Some sort of group instinct or osmosis," Carter guessed. "Quite fascinating."

"Okay to fry them now?" Howard said.

"Be my guest."

Bringing the Thunderbolt to a stop, the major hovered. He flicked a red switch and remarked, "Powering up the electromagnetic emitter. We should be able to get them all with the first burst."

"Can I do the honors, sir?" Sergeant Kline requested.

"Those bugs give me the creeps."

"They're crustaceans, Sergeant, not arthropods or arachnids," Carter corrected him.

Major Howard descended until the Thunderbolt was barely ten meters above the ground.

"Now, sir?" Sergeant Kline said.

Major Howard nodded. "Show them why they shouldn't mess with us."

The noncom smiled and pressed a button.

By now, Archard had become used to the craft's perpetual humming. Suddenly, it became twice as loud. His skin prickled as if from a heat rash, and his eardrums began to hurt.

Outside, there was a bright flash. Crackling lines of energy enmeshed the Martian and they dropped where they stood.

"Serves them right," Sergeant Kline said.

The planetary scientist tapped a finger on his armrest.

"Let's move on. We have three more farms to check."

"Let's hope they don't attack the colony before we get back," Major Howard said.

"I deem that unlikely after our display of power," Carter said, and turned toward Archard. "What do you think, Captain Rahn?"

"There's no predicting the Martians," Archard said. "But one thing I do know. Once they're on the move, they don't stop until they've wiped their enemies out."

Carter considered that. "Fly faster, Major Howard."

The Visitor Center at Wellsville was exactly the same as the Visitor Center in New Meridian. The same height---two stories.

The same number of rooms---17. The same L-shape. The same brown color. Which stood to reason since both were constructed from the same molds. To save on costs, every structure on Mars was modular.

The woman who ran the Center wore a nametag identifying her as Carla. In her thirties, she had black hair cut in a bob and wore a bright pink pantsuit, pink socks, and pink shoes.

"You must be very fond of pink," Trisna Sahir commented as she signed the etablet that served as the register.

"It's my favorite color," Carla said. "Has been since I was your daughter's age. How old is she?"

"Four," Trisna said.

"You are a pretty lady," Behula said.

"Thank you," Carla said.

Katla took her turn at signing in. When she was finished, Carla turned the etablet and read the screen.

"You're both from New Meridian? Are you here on holiday?"

"No," Trisna said sadly.

"Oh. I hope it's not a health issue. Patients come from both of the other colonies to see Dr. Fields at our hospital. He's the best on Mars."

"No, not health," Trisna said.

Clearly curious, Carla said, "If I can be of any assistance, you have only to let me know." She took a room key card from a row of slots on the wall behind her. "Same room for both of you or would you care for separate rooms?"

"Separate," Katla said.

Carla plucked another key card from a slot. "Is your luggage outside?"

"No luggage," Katla said.

"You came all the way from New Meridian and you didn't bring anything with you?"

"We'll get by," Katla said.

"Remarkable." Carla came around the counter. "But then, this is an unusual day."

"How so?" Katla asked.

"There was a special report on the news about ten minutes ago," Carla related, and indicated a vid screen inset into the wall. "Two people have gone missing." She laughed and shook her head. "Now I ask you. How in the world does a person go missing inside of a dome? Well, two domes, but you see my point, right?"

Katla and Trisna swapped glances.

"It's not as if they can up and vanish into thin air," Carla said.

"Did the newscast say who they are?" Katla asked.

"Yes, but I don't remember their names. I only caught the tail end of the report," Carla said. "One was a man from the Maintenance Center and the other was a woman who works at the Broadcast Center."

Trisna went slightly pale. "Maintenance men are always going down into the tunnels and conduits to repair things. And the Broadcast Center is the heart of the colony's communications."

About to lead them to the elevator, Carla said, "Yes. So?"

"So nothing," Katla said. "She was just making small talk."

"Ah," Carla said, and beckoned. "If you don't mind my saying so, ladies, you people from New Meridian are weird."

CHAPTER 15

The Thunderbolt was approaching the last of the farms when Sergeant Kline, who was riveted to the sensor display, excitedly called out, "Heat signatures, sir."

"How many?" Major Howard said as he began their descent.

Archard could see the display from where he sat. It widened and enlarged as Kline zoomed in, the heat sigs standing out in red.

"Three," Sergeant Kline said. "Two in the house. The third is down in the agripod."

Kylo Carter smiled. "Finally. A stroke of luck. The Martians haven't struck here yet."

"They could at any moment," Archard pointed out. He scanned the rocky landscape but didn't detect any sign of them. Which wasn't all that reassuring.

"We should extract these people, Major," Carter was saying. "We've made good time and can spare a few minutes."

"Consider it done," Howard said, and turned to Sergeant Kline. "Get into an EVA suit and I'll drop you off. As soon as you bring them out, I'll land again and take you on board."

Kline unstrapped and rose from his seat.

"Why land twice?" Carter said.

"It will take him a good ten minutes," Major Howard said. "And I don't think it would be smart to keep this bird on the ground that long."

Archard agreed. The Thunderbolt was less vulnerable in the air. "It will go quicker if I help. The sergeant can take the house, and I'll go down into the growing area."

"It's fine by me if Mr. Carter is all right with it," Major Howard said.

The planetary scientist looked at Archard. "I'd rather not risk losing you. You're our expert on these matters."

"I doubt I've learned much you don't already know," Archard said. In fact, he suspected that the government knew more than

Carter had revealed. "And those people need rescuing before the Martians show up."

"I suppose," Carter said, and nodded. "Very well. But be quick about it."

Unstrapping, Archard joined Sergeant Kline over at the rack of EVA suits. They were military issue, more lightweight than civilian suits, and easier to don. He shrugged and tugged into his, and did a quick systems check. His breather was functioning as it should.

Next to the suit rack was a recessed arms compartment that contained six Individual Combat Weapons, standard issue for United Nations forces. In the old days, it would be called an assault rifle, but the ICW was much more. The butt, the chamber, the fore end grip, and most of the barrel were sheathed in polymer, with a slot at the bottom for the magazine and a feed tube for grenades. On the side was a selector button, controlled by an internal microchip that let troopers choose between 5.56 mm rounds, frag grenades, and incendiaries.

Sergeant Kline opened the compartment, took out an ICW, and offered it to Archard. "Here you go, sir. Let's lock and load."

"Gladly," Archard said. Truth to tell, he'd been uneasy about being unarmed. He slapped in a magazine, slid extras into external pockets on his EVA suit, and loaded up on grenades.

"About to touch down," Major Howard announced.

The Thunderbolt settled so lightly, Archard barely felt it. He moved to the rear airlock and Sergeant Kline followed.

Major Howard swiveled in his chair. "Gentleman, I don't need to remind you, do I, that once I take to the air, there's not a lot I can do if the Martians swarm you. I can't fire if you're close to them or you'll be fried, too."

"Understood, sir," Sergeant Kline said.

"And you, Captain?"

Archard hefted his ICW and smiled. "Let's do this."

As usual, the airlock seemed to take forever to cycle. Exchanging atmospheres was a complex procedure. The pumps, the blowers, the critical ratio of gases, everything had to be just right.

Archard waited impatiently for the panel to show green. Beside him, Sergeant Kline was feeding frag grenades into his ICW.

"You've fought these things before, sir. Any tips you can give me?"

"They're fast and they're tough," Archard said.

Sergeant Kline paused with a grenade in his hand. "That's it?"

"Single shots are never enough to put one down," Archard elaborated. "On full auto, you're just wasting ammo, so three-round bursts are best. Aim at the middle of the carapace on the small pink ones. And try not to let them get within three meters. They can jump that far. Maybe further."

Kline grinned. "That's better, sir. What about the big blue things like the one I saw you fighting?"

"They're something else entirely," Archard said. "You can unload a magazine into one and it won't go down. Your best bet is a frag in its face."

"I hear that," Kline said, and finished loading his grenade tube. "Anything else?"

"You already know they don't have heat sigs," Archard said. "Keep your motion sensor at max. And remember, nine times out of ten they come at you from underground. Even with the motion sensor, you might not have much warning."

"Wonderful," Sergeant Kline said.

There was a click and the control light turned green. The outer door slowly slid wide, filling the airlock with the pale glare of the Martian sun.

"Good luck, sir," Kline said as they emerged.

"You too."

They separated, the noncom jogging toward the house module, Archard making for the agripod. The military's EVA suits were streamlined so their movements weren't restricted, and in the Red Planet's lesser gravity, a trooper could run twice as fast as on Earth.

Archard's helmet filled with Major Howard's voice.

"Gentlemen, be advised that the family's name is Parkhill. Husband is Frank. Wife is Lydia. They have a twelve-year-old daughter, Mandy."

"Roger that," Archard said, and broke into long bounds to cover the fifty meters swiftly. At the pod bubble, he tapped in the U.N.I.C. override code. In case of emergencies, it enabled U.N.I.C. personnel to enter any structure on Mars.

Once again, he had to wait for the airlock. As he stepped into the pod, he saw a civilian EVA suit hanging on the wall. Ahead was a stairwell leading below. Stairs were used instead of an elevator because each use of electricity was a drain on a farm's generator.

To the left of the stairs was a freight lift, but they were used exclusively for bringing crops to the surface at harvest time and for taking equipment below.

Archard took the stairs two at a hop. At the bottom, it was like stepping into a whole new world. Before him spread acre after acre of green plant life. Climate controlled, the farms produced crops year-round. Wheat, corn, oats, vegetables, and more.

Few sights on Mars made Archard as homesick as an agrifarm. It brought to mind Earth with her lush tropical jungles and her thriving forests and verdant plains. Compared to Mars, Earth was the Garden of Eden.

Archard checked the heat signature on his helmet display. Whoever was down there was two acres away, on his left, in a field of corn. He increased the volume on his suit's external speaker and called out, "Attention. This is Captain Archard Rahn of U.N.I.C. Mr. Parkhill, is that you? Come out, please. We're here to evacuate your family."

The tops of corn stalks swayed as someone hurried along the rows.

Archard's motion sensors gave a slight ping. A ripple had appeared at the limits of the unit's range. "Hurry, please," he shouted.

Out of the corn burst the farmer. Only it wasn't Mr. Parkhill. It was the Mrs., a young woman in her twenties, dressed in overalls and a work shirt. Her worry was transparent.

"What was that about an evacuation? Is my family in danger?"

Before Archard could answer, the floor between them erupted in a clamorous shower of debris.

CHAPTER 16

The restaurant was called *Barsoom*. Katla vaguely recalled the name had something to do with a famous writer of long ago who penned a series about Mars. She was more interested in the menu and decided on a *Dejah Thoris* burger.

"I'm glad they gave us the vouchers," Trisna Sahir commented after the waitress took their orders and walked off. "I have a lot of things I need to buy for Behula and myself."

Katla wasn't feeling nearly as grateful toward the government, not after her talk with Chief Administrator Reubens. She supposed she shouldn't be surprised that the world's leaders misled everyone. Politicians had been lording it over the people they were elected to serve since forever.

"You've been unusually quiet. Is everything all right?"

"Fine," Katla fibbed. To change the subject, she glanced at Piotr Zabinskis, seated beside her, and then over at Behula, who was across from him. "These two are about done in. We need to get them to bed early."

"I intend to turn in early, myself," Trisna said, resting her elbows on the table. "I didn't sleep well the entire time we were in the tank. I was too afraid the Martians would find us."

"We're safe enough at the moment," Katla said to ease the worry that blossomed in Piotr's eyes.

"You heard that lady at the Visitor Center," Trisna said. "Two people have gone missing. Wasn't that how it started at New Meridian? With missing people?"

"Some farmers, yes," Katla remembered Archard telling her.

"I couldn't go through the horrors of New Meridian a second time. Could you?"

No, Katla wouldn't want to. Not in a million lifetimes. But she had to face facts. It was very likely the Martians now knew about Wellsville. And if so, the second colony could be in for the same nightmare New Meridian suffered.

"You look upset," Trisna said.

"Me? No." Katla smiled and shook her head. Putting her hand on Piotr's, she lightly tousled his hair. "And you, mister, can lose that frown. You should be happy the worst is over." She felt terrible deceiving him, but he had been through hell and back again, and she would spare him as long as possible.

A TV on the wall was airing a nature documentary about the African veldt. Shows about Earth were immensely popular on Mars. The screen showed antelope being stalked by a lioness. Suddenly, the image dissolved into random lines and dashes, and then the face of a newsman. At the same time, the TV emitted a series of loud beeps.

Everyone in the restaurant stopped what they were doing and turned toward the TV.

"Citizens of Wellsville. This is Clive Owlsley for W. N. News. We're sorry to interrupt your regular programming, but Chief Administrator Evander Reubens has an important special announcement to make. Please stand by."

"This can't be good," Trisna said.

Captain Archard Rahn glimpsed a huge form in the midst of the billowing cloud of dust and the shower of broken floor bits. A driller, he called them, enormous Martians capable of boring through the ground at incredible speed. The drillers were responsible for the network of tunnels the Martians used to get around. He saw the serrated ridges at the crown of its head stop spinning and a pair of eye stalks rise into the air. The eyes swung toward him, and in the time it would take him to blink his, the driller vanished down the tunnel it had made.

"Captain Rahn? Are you still there?"

Mrs. Parkhill's panicked cry galvanized Archard into running to reach her before the Martians did. His EVA suit spared him from the swirling dust, and his sensors enabled him to avoid the gaping hole in a floor designed to withstand a Magnitude 10 earthquake. "Mrs. Parkhill, don't move! I'm coming to get you." Her heat signature was like a red beacon on his helmet display.

She was swatting at the dust and coughing. "What was that awful thing? What's going on? I don't understand."

Archard was glad she was staying relatively calm, given the circumstances. "I don't have time to explain except to say that your farm is under attack by Martians."

"But there aren't any…" she began, and stopped.

"We have to get you into your EVA suit," Archard said. "I'll guide you." He went to put an arm around her shoulders, but she suddenly pointed and yelled.

"Lookout!"

Archard spun.

Martians were scrambling out of the hole, the pinkish-red creatures that resembled crabs. The eyes of those nearest swung in their direction and the creatures flexed their grippers, and attacked.

Planting himself between them and Mrs. Parkhill, Archard cut loose with his ICW. As he had instructed Sergeant Kline, he aimed at the middle of their upper carapace, where Kylo Carter said the heart was located. His first three-round burst dropped a creature cold. He killed a second, a third. More appeared behind them.

"Back up!" Archard shouted, and backpedaled. He felt Mrs. Parkhill's hand on his shoulder, heard her frightened breaths close to his earpiece.

"My family! My husband and daughter!"

"They're being tended to," was all Archard had time to say. Then the Martians were on them. He raked half a dozen with controlled bursts, momentarily clearing the aisle. Switching to frag grenades, he fired one into the tunnel.

"Get down!" he bellowed, and pulled Mrs. Parkhill with him as he dropped onto his shoulder.

The explosion spewed more dust into the air, along with Martian body parts. No more poured out of the tunnel.

Wasting no time, Archard hauled Mrs. Parkhill to her feet. "We have to move!" He pulled her with him, skirting the tunnel with his ICW trained on its dark maw.

"I don't believe this!" Mrs. Parkhill exclaimed. "How can this be happening?"

"It's happening," Archard said, and pushed her ahead of him. "Go on. Get topside and into your suit." He covered them, expecting more Martians to emerge. Strangely, none did.

As he reached the foot of the stairs, his helmet crackled.

"What's going on down there, Captain?" Major Howard snapped. "I need a sitrep."

"I have Mrs. Parkhill," Archard reported. "What about the others?"

"Sergeant Kline is bringing the husband and the girl. They just came out of the house. Hurry it up. My motions sensors are going crazy."

"On our way," Archard said.

Mrs. Parkhill was sealing her EVA suit when Archard rejoined her. "Stay close and do exactly as I say."

"My family?"

"We have them."

"Thank God."

Keeping an eye on the stairs, Archard activated the airlock. He didn't understand why the Martians weren't after them. The creatures had one attack mode and one attack mode only; full-bore.

"I have so many questions," Mrs. Parkhill said.

"Not now."

They entered the airlock. Archard endured another interminable wait, his nerves on raw edge. When the outer door opened, he gripped Mrs. Parkhill by the arm and broke into a sprint.

Off near the house, Sergeant Kline and the father and daughter were hastening toward the rendezvous point.

The Thunderbolt was on its landing approach.

Archard smiled, thinking that maybe, just maybe, they would get out of there with their hides intact. He should have known better.

Over a low rise to the north swept a wave of Martians.

CHAPTER 17

All eyes in the *Barsoom* were glued to the large TV screen on the wall. Except for a few whispers, an expectant silence had fallen. Special Announcements by Chief Administrators were rare. Everyone present sensed that something important was in the wind.

Katla looked around. No one appeared particularly worried, though. They should be. If she was right, they were in for a hellstorm of horror.

Trisna bent toward her and whispered, "Do you think he will tell them about the Martians?"

"If he has any brains, he will."

The newsman had a finger to an ear and was listening to someone off-camera. He nodded, then announced, "I give you Chief Administrator Evander Reubens."

The scene shifted to an imposing office, and to C.A. Reubens seated behind his desk, smiling. "My fellow Wellsvillians," he began. "I apologize for this intrusion into your day. In a few short minutes, the emergency sirens will sound. When you hear them, please proceed immediately to your home or work station, if you are not already at either, and remain there until the sirens sound again to signal the all-clear."

"He's going to tell them!" Trisna whispered.

Katla wasn't so sure.

"As you might have heard in earlier new reports," Reubens continued, "two individuals have gone missing. You might be wondering how that can possibly happen in contained environments like our bio domes. We were wondering the same thing, and now we have an explanation."

"Here it comes," Trisna said excitedly.

"Gas," Reubens said.

Trisna straightened. "What?"

"Our Maintenance Center personnel have discovered a gas leak," Chief Administrator Reubens said. "As some of you are well aware, we use certain liquefied gases in various chemical processes in the routine operation of our colony. I'm sorry to report there has been a break in a line."

"A gas leak," Katla said in disgust.

On the screen, Reubens was holding out his hands in a gesture of reassurance. "There's nothing to worry about. The leak is minor, and we expect to have it repaired and everything back to normal before the sun goes down."

"That's only a couple of hours," a male customer remarked.

"In the meantime, for your own protection, and until we verify that the gas hasn't spread farther, I would like all of you to stay indoors where you'll be safe."

Happy voices broke out in the restaurant. Someone joked about smelling gas and others laughed.

"So once more, when you hear the sirens, report to your work station or go home." The camera zoomed in on Reubens and his smile widened. "I thank you for your time, and apologize again for the inconvenience."

"He is slick, that one," Trisna said.

"He's a lying bastard," Katla said.

Piotr stirred beside her. "My mom always said that's a bad word."

Katla turned, about to respond that she wasn't his mother, but she held her tongue. The boy looked so miserable, she hugged him. "I'm sorry, Piotr. But that man is lying to these people, and it makes me mad."

"My mom said lying was bad, too." Piotr's eyes moistened and he sniffled.

Katla didn't want him to start crying again. Not that she blamed him. If she had lost both her parents at his age, she would be a mess, too.

"Where do we go?" Trisna said. "The Visitor Center?"

"We don't have anywhere else," Katla said. She dearly wanted to visit the hospital and talk to its director about being reassigned, but that would have to wait.

The waitress hurried over with their food on a tray. "You'll have to eat fast," she said as she set the plates down. "We're closing as soon as the sirens sound."

"How about if we take it to go?" Katla suggested.

"I'll bring containers," the waitress said, and hurried off.

"Could we be wrong, Dr. Dkany?" Trisna said. "Could it really be a gas leak?"

"I'm ninety-nine percent sure it isn't," Katla said.

Trisna sadly shook her head. "These poor people. Too bad we can't do anything."

Katla gave a mild start. There *was* something she could do. If it got her arrested, so what? The lives of the colonists were more important. "I have an idea," she said.

Archard didn't need to tell Mrs. Parkhill to run like hell. At the sight of the Martians, she did.

The creatures were still a ways off when Sergeant Kline reached the extraction point. Motioning the husband and the girl behind him, he faced the charging Martians, and at extreme range, let fly with a fragmentation grenade.

The bright flash of the blast produced only a low *krump*. On Mars, even the loudest of sounds could barely be heard a hundred meters away.

The Martians slowed, then came on as fast as before.

Archard estimated there had to be fifty creatures, or better, in the cluster flowing toward the noncom and those he was protecting. Far too many for a single trooper to overcome.

Sergeant Kline fired another frag. This time, the grenade struck amid the foremost creatures and blew several into oblivion.

The Thunderbolt continued to descend.

Behind Archard, Lydia Parkhill hollered, "Frank! Mandy! Mommy is on her way!"

The Martians were splitting up, some bearing right, others left. Plainly, they intended to envelop Kline and the farmer and his child in a pincer movement.

Archard let go of Mrs. Parkhill. Taking a long bound, he jumped as high as he could. At the apex, he wedged his ICW to his shoulder and lobbed a frag of his own. He aimed at the Martians breaking to the left and was pleased to see several go down in a wild thrashing of limbs.

Over the commlink came a bellow from Major Howard, "Hold on! Another sixty seconds and we'll be down."

Kline began firing grenades at the Martians on the right.

Archard covered the last ten meters in a sprint. Drawing up short, he was taking aim when Mandy Parkhill screamed and pointed, and the father shouted, "No!"

Unnoticed by Archard, Lydia Parkhill had dropped behind. She was severely winded, and was holding a hand to her side.

A pair of Martians had spotted her. Pulling ahead of the rest, they scrambled toward her with astonishing speed.

"Save her!" Mandy screeched.

Archard raced flat-out. He switched to armor-piercing rounds and triggered a burst that caught the foremost creature in the side but didn't seem to have any effect.

Lydia Parkhill tripped and fell.

"Mom!" Mandy wailed.

Kicking off with his right foot, Archard fired in midair. This time, his rounds penetrated just below the creature's eye stalks. The thing lurched, took a couple more steps, and collapsed.

The mother's terror-struck face was riveted to the other creature. Paralyzed with fear, she made no attempt to rise from her knees.

"Run!" Archard roared. He might as well have saved his breath.

The other Martian was still a good five meters from her when an extra surge of adrenaline brought Archard to the woman's side. He fired on full auto, and when his magazine went dry, ejected it and slapped in a new one. It wasn't needed. The Martian sprawled in a heap, convulsed, and was still.

Grabbing Lydia's wrist, Archard pulled her toward Kline and the others.

The Thunderbolt was almost to them, its undercarriage practically brushing the ground.

The remaining Martians were closing fast.

It was a toss-up which would reach them first, the aircraft or the creatures.

A spurt of the propulsion drive, and Major Howard won. In an exceptional display of his piloting ability, Howard turned the

Thunderbolt when it was almost upon them so that as it came to a stop, the open outer airlock door was almost within arm's reach.

"Get on board!" Archard commanded the family. "Go! Go! Go!" To gain them precious seconds, he poured lead into the Martians.

Sergeant Kline did the same.

In a twinkling, the Parkhills were all in the airlock.

Archard gestured at Kline and followed him in, smacking the cycle control. Side-by-side, they crouched in the opening. Side-by-side, they poured lead into the charging creatures as the door closed all-too-slowly.

Nine or ten Martians were down kicking when Kline had to stop firing because the outer door was in his way. Another moment, and Archard had to let up on his trigger, as well. Only when the door thunked shut and he felt the Thunderbolt rising did he let out the breath he hadn't realized he was holding.

"We did it," Sergeant Kline said quietly, as if he couldn't quite believe they had.

Archard was about to compliment him when their comms blared.

"Captain Rahn! Sergeant Kline! In here, quickly," Kylo Carter said. "I've just received word from Chief Administrator Reubens. Wellsville might be under attack."

COLONY DOWN

CHAPTER 18

"I wish you had gone back to the Visitor Center like I asked," Katla said as she hurried along Pohl Avenue. Blocks off reared the four-story Broadcast Center, one of the highest structures in Wellsville. "And taken the children with you," she added. Piotr was clinging fast to her left hand.

Trisna had Behula in her arms. Because of her shorter legs, she took two steps for each of Katla's. "Where you go, we go. If you are right about the missing people, it would not do to be separated. Is that not so, Piotr?"

"Please don't leave me," Piotr said to Katla. "You promised you wouldn't."

Katla felt a twinge of guilt. The boy had a knack for tugging at her heartstrings. "You would be better off at the Center. We're not supposed to be out on the street."

"There are still a lot of people about," Trisna mentioned.

The sirens had sounded about five minutes ago, and the colony's citizenry were doing as they had been instructed and hastening home or to their work station.

"If we're stopped by soldiers, what will we say?" Trisna said.

Katla sighed. Her friend was a born worrier if ever there was one. "We haven't seen any troopers yet."

"Let us hope we don't," Trisna said.

By the time they reached the Broadcast Center, the streets were nearly empty. Katla held one of the wide doors for Trisna and Piotr.

A spacious lobby was decorated with paintings of Earth scenes. Here and there were potted artificial plants. The receptionist sat at a desk typing on her computer. In her twenties, her dreadlocks were adorned with tiny gold tassels, the latest fashion. She looked up in some surprise, her eyebrows arching. "Yes? May I help you?"

"We need to speak to whoever is in charge," Katla said.

"That would be Mr. Cain. But I'm afraid that's quite impossible."

"It's imperative," Katla said.

The younger woman raised her fingers from her keyboard. "I'm sorry, but haven't you heard? The chief administrator has asked that everyone either return home or report to where they work."

"Forget that," Katla said. "I really must see Mr. Cain."

"Who *are* you?" the receptionist asked.

Katla gave her name and, "I'm a physician and exobiologist, and what I have to say is of critical importance."

"I don't know," the receptionist said uncertainly. "I suppose I could ring his secretary and let her know and she can take it from there."

"That would be fine, yes."

"Wait over there, if you please." The receptionist indicated a row of chairs.

"What if they don't believe you?" Trisna said as they went over.

"I have you to corroborate everything," Katla said.

Trisna snorted. "I am no one special. I worked in the Supply Center in New Meridian. In their eyes, I will not count for much."

"You're too humble."

"I am Hindu. Humble is what we do."

To Katla's relief, they weren't kept waiting long. An elevator dinged and out strode two men in expensive suits and polished shoes. The taller of the men had an arrogant bearing about him.

"Mr. Cain, I presume?" Katla said, rising to offer her hand.

"Dr. Dkany, is it?" Cain said, and gave Trisna and the children a puzzled look. "You must be new. I thought I knew all the doctors on the hospital staff."

"I'm from New Meridian," Katla enlightened him.

"That explains it," Cain said, and indicated the other man. "This is Mr. Jennings, my Executive Assistant." Cain smiled at her. "How may I help you, Doctor?"

"I don't quite know where to begin, so I'll jump right in," Katla said. "New Meridian has fallen. It's been overrun by Martians. Nearly all the colonists were massacred. Torn to pieces and left where they fell."

"Except for their heads," Trisna said nervously. "The Martians always take the heads."

Katla went to say more, but Cain held up a hand and stared at her and then at Trisna and back again.

"What is this, ladies? Some sort of joke?"

"No, I assure you," Katla began, only to have Cain cut her off.

"Martians, you say? And they've overrun the third colony?" Cain glanced at his companion, who shook his head and chuckled. "Are you insane, ladies? Are you drunk? Or high? Why would you foist this nonsense on me?"

"Listen, please," Katla said. "I'm deadly serious. New Meridian is lost. And the Martians are about to do the same to Wellsville. Those two men who have gone missing? The Martians are responsible. You have to go on the air and warn everyone. You have to let them know what they're up against."

"Dr. Dkany," Cain said, shaking his head. "Enough. I won't listen to any more of this nonsense. I'm a busy man."

Katla clutched at his sleeve as he turned to go. "Please. You have to hear me out."

"Wellsville is under a curfew, madam," Cain said. "I suggest you and your friend get to where you should be and leave pranks like this to those the boy's age." He jerked his arm loose. "Jennings, show these ladies out. If they give you any trouble, call the Security Center and have the U.N.I.C. deal with them."

"Yes, sir," Jennings said. He was thin with black hair, and didn't hide his resentment. "Leave peacefully, ladies, right this moment. Or else."

Katla started to go after Cain, but Jennings barred her way.

"I won't tell you twice, Doctor."

Katla hesitated.

Jennings suddenly grabbed Piotr by the arm and hauled him toward the wide glass doors.

"Hold on!" Katla said, going after them.

Ignoring her, Jennings shoved a door open and guided Piotr through. He let go and stepped back and gestured for Katla and Trisna to join Piotr outside.

"How dare you," Katla fumed. Brushing by him, she clasped Piotr's hand, planning to go right back in and confront Cain whether he or his assistant liked it or not.

The door closed behind her. Jennings touched a pad on the wall and there was a loud click.

Katla pulled on the handle but the door wouldn't open. She pulled harder, then angrily shook the handle.

Jennings grinned and waved, to rub it in, then walked away.

"He has locked us out," Trisna said. "That man is mean through and through."

Katla would have vented her spleen if not for the children.

Turning from the building, Trisna gasped. "Look! We took too long!"

For as far as Katla could see, the streets were empty. An uneasy feeling came over her but she made light of their situation by saying, "Relax, will you? Everything is fine."

"No," Trisna said. "It isn't."

Archard removed his helmet and held it under his arm when he emerged from the Thunderbolt's airlock. There weren't enough seats for everyone, so Sergeant Kline let the girl, Mandy, have his. Archard motioned for the mother to take his. Frank Parkhill remained standing.

"ETA," Kylo Carter said to Major Howard. The planetary scientist was drumming his fingers on his armrest.

"At max speed," the major said, "forty-seven minutes."

"Damn," Carter said.

"You received a message from Chief Administrator Reubens?" Archard said.

Carter nodded. "Two colonists have gone missing. And a maintenance tunnel camera caught an image of something before it went dark. Reubens has ordered everyone indoors under the pretext of a gas leak."

Archard felt the blood drain from his face. "It's the worst thing he could do."

Both Carter and Major Howard turned to look at him.

"How's that again, Captain?" the major said.

"It's what I did at New Meridian," Archard explained. "As the top U.N.I.C. officer there, under Article Three, Section B, of the Colonization Protocols, I assumed emergency command and ordered everyone indoors."

"Prudent of you," Carter said.

"Stupid of me," Archard said. "Martian combat tactics aren't like ours. They live underground. They move through tunnels they bore themselves. That's how they overran New Meridian. By going from house to house, building to building, and coming up from below."

"Are you saying they can bore right through a building module?" Major Howard said, incredulous. "Those modules are strong enough to withstand a grenade blast at close range."

"That's exactly what I'm saying," Archard said. "Your C.A. has made it easy for the Martians by having all the chickens go into their coops. Now the foxes can kill as they please."

"A crude analogy, but…" Kylo Carter gnawed his bottom lip. "Major, raise Administrator Reubens for me, would you?"

"Right away, sir."

"What is all this?" Lydia Parkhill asked. "What in the world is going on?"

"Haven't you figured it out yet, hon?" her husband said. "Mars is inhabited. And the inhabitants don't want us here."

"Succinctly put, Mr. Parkhill," Carter said.

"But Earth has had colonies for over a century," Lydia said. "How could we not know there were Martians?"

"I have C.A. Reubens on the line," Major Howard announced.

"Put him on speaker," Carter said.

Archard was thinking of Katla. Of how much she had come to mean to him. He barely noticed the sound of static that preceded Chief Administrator Reubens' voice.

"…Carter? Are you there?"

"I'm here, Evander," Carter said. "We're on our way in, but it will be a while before we get there. I'd like an update, please. What is your current situation?"

"I have everything under control," Reubens said. "Everyone has been ordered indoors. I had Lieutenant Burroughs send two troopers with the maintenance personnel searching for the worker who went missing, and they didn't find a thing. The same at the Broadcast Center."

"No Martians?" Archard said without thinking. As he knew all too well, a favorite tactic of theirs was to kill someone so that others would investigate and in turn be attacked.

"Who was that?" Reubens said.

"Captain Archard Rahn from New Meridian," Carter said.

"Ah. No, Captain. No Martians," Reubens said. "The soldiers and the crews returned safely."

"Strange," Archard said. "The Martians must be up to something new."

"Whatever they have planned, I'm sure we can deal with it," Reubens said. "Counting your two men from New Meridian, I have seven troopers at my disposal. Ten, when the major and you and Sergeant Kline arrive. Plus your RAM battle suit and the one our own security force has, and three tanks."

"It's not enough," Archard said bleakly.

"Nonsense," Chief Administrator Reubens declared. "You were overrun at New Meridian because you only had four troopers and no idea what you were up against. We have more soldiers and more equipment and we're better prepared."

"That we are, sir," Major Howard said.

"Now if you'll excuse me, I have an invasion to forestall," Reubens said.

The screen dissolved into lines and squiggles.

Kylo Carter swiveled toward Archard. "In your estimation, how much damage can the Martians inflict in the forty minutes or so it will take us to get there?"

Archard gave it to him straight. "If they wanted to, they could destroy the entire colony."

CHAPTER 19

Levlin Winslow scuttled along a dark tunnel with Nilista at his side. Ahead and behind flowed a river of Martians, part of a vast force converging on the colony of Wellsville.

He supposed he should feel guilty about taking part in the gathering, as the Martians referred to it. But he didn't. God help him---not that there was a God---but he didn't feel a shred of shame, regret or misgiving. The only emotions he felt were a sense of excitement and delight.

Winslow had never been so happy in his life. All the cares and woes of his former existence had been washed away by the new sensations his changed state had brought about.

As if to demonstrate that fact, Nilista's consciousness merged with his. *"You are mistaken, my bindmate."*

"In what way?"

"That which you call God we revere as the Source of All. The Source is in all of us. In you. In me. In the fullness of the Unity."

"I would never have expected it of your people." That last was a slip of the tongue. Winslow meant to say 'species.'

"Thank you for acknowledging we are fellow sentients. And need I remind you that you are one of us now? We are your people."

"But to believe in God…"

"How can we not? You have experienced the Unity, and the Unity stems from the Source. You have felt our conscious selves joined in totality. The many become one. And from our union, harmony results. From harmony, inner peace, and a long and joy-filled life."

Her comment sparked a question. *"I never thought to ask. How long are our life spans?"*

"These bodies last an average of nine hundred of your Earth years," Nilista answered. *"At which time we can choose to be provided with another or merge with the Source."*

Winslow was so startled, he stumbled. He would have fallen had he not grabbed at the side of the tunnel, and stopped.

Nilista stopped, too, and came to him. The other Martians veered around, paying no attention whatsoever. *"What is wrong, my bindmate?"*

"Did I understand you right?" Winslow projected in astonishment. *"I'm going to live nine hundred years?"*

"Nine thousand should you so wish. Few do. After two or three thousand, most are eager to advance their sentience to the next level."

"Nine thousand?" Winslow inwardly repeated in a daze.

"I feel your emotions are in a whirl. What is the cause?"

Winslow laughed. Without a mouth, without lips, he laughed and laughed until Nilista took hold of his carapace with both her grippers and shook him.

"What is this strange behavior? Has the exchange gone awry?"

"No, no," Winslow assured her. With an effort, he smothered his mirth. *"Nilista. Nilista. My sweet, wonderful bindmate. You have made me the happiest sentient alive."*

"I have?"

Winslow sensed that she was extremely pleased but also confused. *"My lifespan in my other form would have been barely ninety years. Now, thanks to your scientists and your incredible technology, I'll live forever."*

"No one lives that long."

"Nine hundred years or nine thousand, you have no idea of the gift you've given me."

"You truly are happy, then?"

"I have never, ever been happier," Winslow thought, and realized it was true.

"And you are not troubled at taking part in the harvest of heads?"

"What's to be troubled about?" Winslow replied. *"We're not really killing anyone. We're taking the heads so their sentiences can be transferred into new bodies. And then they can live as long as we do. We're doing them a favor and they don't even know it."*

"An excellent way to look at it, yes. Now open yourself to the Unity. Feel what we feel and think what we think. Relish this

opportunity for your former fellows to experience the same happiness."

Winslow laughed. "*I'll relish the hell out of it.*"

Katla's nerves were jangling. It was eerie, walking along the deserted streets, the entire colony as quiet as an Earth cemetery.

Piotr Zabinski must have felt the same because his hand tightened in hers.

"We're all right," Katla sought to comfort him, yet again. "We'll go to the Visitor Center and stay put until they signal the all-clear."

Trisna was rocking Behula in her arms and whispering in Hindi.

Katla was sorry she'd gone to the Broadcast Center. She should have known how they'd react. To Cain and everyone else who had never seen one, the idea of Martians existing was preposterous. Not once in all the years the three colonies existed had anyone encountered a Martian. Until now.

"I have the feeling people are looking out their windows at us," Trisna said.

Katla scanned the mix of homes and businesses on both sides of the street. All the windows in the house modules were tinted so those inside could see out but no one could see in.

"Maybe they are. Who cares?"

"You would think someone would offer to take us in," Trisna said. "There is such a thing as the cup of human kindness."

"Hindus believe in that?" Katla absently asked.

"My dear Doctor, kindness is the very essence of

Hindu belief. We were doing until others long before you Westerners stole the saying from us."

Katla saw Trisna was grinning, and laughed. "My specialties are medicine and science, not religion, but I seem to remember that a lot of them teach the Golden Rule."

"And who do you think started that?" Trisna said, chortling.

Little Behula raised her head and smiled.

Piotr, too, smiled. He was visibly relaxing now that the adults were more at ease.

Katla kept it going with, "Aren't Hindus the ones who worship cows?" She winked at Piotr and said "Moo!" and he laughed for the first time in days.

"You silly Westerners," Trisna said. "We do not worship them. We respect them, as we do all forms of life."

"Monkeys, too, right?" Katla said. "I seem to recall that you respect them so much, you let them breed like rabbits. To where there were so many, they nearly drove you out of your own cities."

"Well, monkeys will be monkeys," Trisna said, and perfectly imitated the sound a monkey might make.

All four of them were laughing as they went around a corner, and all four of them abruptly stopped at the sight of a pair of soldiers.

"Oh, no," Trisna gasped.

"They're going the other way. They don't see us." Katla moved toward the recessed doorway to a clothing store with a CLOSED sign glowing in the window.

"Hurry. In here."

Dashing down the steps, they stood in the shadows.

Katla rose onto her toes to peer out, Piotr clinging to her leg.

Trisna tried to set Behula down, but the girl shook her head and wrapped her arms tight around her mother's neck. "What will they do if they catch us? Arrest us?"

"That's the least of our worries," Katla said, and could have kicked herself. The children were downcast again. Their good spirits had evaporated.

"Do you think the Martians will wait until dark to attack like they did at New Meridian?"

Since the children were already scared again, Katla saw no harm in saying, "They broke into the maintenance tunnels there well before the sun went down."

"I didn't know that," Trisna said. "But the main attack was not until nightfall, am I right?"

Horrific images of the slaughter at the hospital made Katla grimace. "Yes."

"Then we have a few hours."

We hope, Katla thought. The truth was, at that very moment, the creatures could be boring up under every building in the colony and they wouldn't know it. She glanced up at the golden dome, the apex of Earth technology, touted as impenetrable to everything except a nuclear strike. Perhaps that was true. But the geniuses who designed the domes never imagined that an enemy might penetrate a colony from below. And now look. One colony down, and the second in peril.

"A ruby for your thoughts," Trisna said.

Katla pointed at the artificial cement under their feet and made a crab-like movement with her free hand.

"Oh," Trisna said.

CHAPTER 20

Levlin Winslow was so happy, he was giddy. Ironic, given that he was about to take part in an attack on a colony established by his home planet. Rather, his *former* home planet. Mars was his home now. Even if he wanted to---which he didn't---he couldn't go back. For one thing, his former body had been ripped apart. For another, the process was one-way.

The swarm he and his bindmate were part of was nearing Wellsville. A few hundred meters more and the tunnel widened into a gigantic cavern filled with thousands of Martians.

"This is where we will wait for the Aryghr to give the signal," Nilista inserted into his consciousness.

"Who?"

Their immediate group veered and halted at the base of the sheer cavern wall. Jumping high, Nilista clung to the vertical face, then began to climb.

Winslow did the same. Above them, the Martians who had already arrived hung by their eight legs in long rows, like so many bats.

Nilista didn't answer his question until she had settled into position. *"I must enlighten you further."*

Amazed at how easily he could cling to smooth rock, Winslow said, *"About?"*

"An Aryghr is our name for what you would call our leader caste, those among us who are yellow."

"How about you and me?"

"Our caste is known as the Gryghr. Your kind call us soldiers, or workers, but we are more of both than either. We are as much of the Unity as the Aryghr, except our functions are different. Do you understand?"

"Yes," Winslow said. *"What about the blues and the browns?"*

"The blue caste are the Hryghr. You think of them as our warriors, and that is half-right. They are also our generals in time of conflict. Our Samson's, as it were."

"You know about Samson?"

"You would be surprised how much we have learned of Blue World cultures and history."

"Let me guess about the brown caste," Winslow projected. *"They are your scientists."*

"Yes. The Eryghr. They perform other functions, as well." Nilista raised her eye stalks so her eyes were close to his. *"While I have called them castes to better help you comprehend, that is not the right way to describe their place in the Unity. Our functions are a consequence of our bodies, not a social state imposed by others. A Hryghr could no more perform the tasks of an Eryghr than we could. Nor could an Eryghr perform ours. Do you comprehend all of this?"*

An old saying popped into Winslow's 'head.' *"Different strokes for different folks."*

"Strokes and folks? I am confused."

"Yes, I comprehend."

"Good."

Winslow wanted to ask her what the giant drillers were called but Nilista's sentience suddenly merged with his.

"We must be silent. Look. A Hryghr has arrived."

Down below, a huge blue Martian had emerged from a tunnel and was moving to the center of the cavern.

"The Hryghr will address us," Nilista said. *"Open yourself to the Unity, as I have taught you. To all the others as well as to me."*

Winslow hadn't quite mastered the technique. He could do it, but it took considerable effort before his receptors were in tune with the rest. The transition was drastic, like slipping into a warm, flowing current, filled with images and symbols and words.

The Hryghr was already 'speaking.'

"...take part in a great and glorious gathering of Blue World sentients. The harvest is small and we are plentiful. They are weak in body and we are strong. But we must not make the same mistakes we made at their other golden egg. We rushed to engage them, believing our numbers were enough, and discovered that though few and fragile, they have power, these Blue Worlders. Not the power of the Unity, as we do. Their power is in their constructs. In their machines, as they call them, and their

weapons. We lost many kindred at that gathering. We must not lose as many here."

The Hryghr stopped, and Winslow felt a swelling of agreement from the assembled Martians.

"This time, we will be wise. We will use craft and guile. While some of us surround their golden eggs to prevent them from escaping, we will bore in under their structures. When we are all in position, the call will be given, and we will burst up upon them and collect their heads for transference."

"Call?" Winslow thought, but Nilista was too engrossed in the Unity to respond.

"Exercise caution, my kindred. Perform as our plan requires and we will prevail. And once we have, once these two golden eggs have fallen, we will put the next phase of our strategy into effect. The Source of All willing, not only will we convert the Blue Worlders on our world to the joy of the Unity, but all those on their world, as well."

Katla didn't budge until the pair of troopers had gone around a corner blocks away. "Let's go," she said, and scooted up the steps.

Piotr kept pace, his eyes wide with the fear that had seldom left him since the death of his parents.

Trisna, as always, held Behula, instead of letting the girl walk. Ever since that terrible night in New Meridian, the mother wouldn't let her child go.

Katla thought of Archard, and hoped she would see him soon. She intended to tell him everything Chief Administrator Reubens had revealed to her. Reubens could take his threat of imprisonment, or worse, and shove it. She detested that man and those like him. Professional politicians who lied and manipulated others for their own ends, the whole time justifying their evil by saying it was for the common good. She would as soon have all of them drown in their own slime.

Lost in her reverie, Katla came to the intersection where the troopers had turned and was about to cross when out of the corner of her eye she caught movement, and stopped short.

The troopers had turned, but they hadn't gone more than a few meters and were standing talking. They saw her and Trisna.

Swallowing her anxiety, Katla turned and smiled. "Hi there. We know we shouldn't be out and about. We're on our back to the Visitor Center."

"Please don't arrest us," Trisna said.

"Dr. Dkany?" one of the soldiers said. "And you, too, Hindu lady?"

The play of sunlight and shadow on their helmet faceplates made it hard to see their faces but Katla recognized the distinct Kentucky drawl.

"Private Everett?"

"And me, as well, Doctor," Private Pasco said cheerfully.

"It is good to see both of you again."

Katla was so glad, she impulsively gripped the Spaniard's arm and pumped it. "Oh, thank heavens it's your two and not Wellsville troopers."

"We *are* Wellsville troopers now," Private Everett said. "Reassigned for the duration of our tours."

"You don't sound very happy about it," Katla said.

Cradling his ICW, the Kentuckian said, "After New Meridian, I just want to go home. None of us should be here."

"*Si*," Private Pasco said. "It is insane what they do. We warned the major. We told him everything."

"What did he say?"

Everett answered. "That we must buck up. That what happened at New Meridian could never happen here. That we're U.N.I.C. and the U.N.I.C. are the toughest mothers anywhere, and we can take whatever the Martians dish out."

"The major is a very foolish man," Private Pasco said.

"I hope they can't hear you," Katla said. She remembered that their commlinks enabled them to stay in constant communication with their headquarters and other troopers.

Pasco grinned. "We switched off our mics and helmet cams the moment we saw you."

"No sense in making trouble for you ladies," Private Everett said.

"We are grateful to both of you," Katla said.

"Yes, we are," Trisna echoed.

Private Everett straightened his lanky frame and looked around. "We'd best escort you to the Visitor Center. No telling who else might come along."

They started off, the troopers on either side, Piotr beaming at Pasco. The boy had taken a liking to the amiable Spaniard during their long trek in the tank.

"Have you seen Captain Rahn?" Katla was eager to learn.

"Not since we got here, no, ma'am," Private Everett said. "They kept him isolated from us."

"But when we were sent out to patrol the streets," Pasco took up the account, "Lieutenant Burroughs told us that the captain went out with the major and some big brain in the Thunderbolt."

"What on earth for?"

"To check on the outlying farmers," Everett said.

"Lieutenant Burroughs is in charge until they return," Pasco said. "She is a good officer, that one."

"Once we get you to the Visitor Center, you stay locked in your rooms, you hear?" Everett said. "Two colonists have gone missing."

"We saw the broadcast," Trisna said.

"Reubens, that lying sack," Everett said. "There's no gas leak. They don't know what happened to those two. But we do."

Private Pasco nodded. "Martians. It has to be."

"Shouldn't we stick together, then?" Trisna said.

"We would love to stay with you," Pasco said, "but if we stay off-line too long, they will send someone to investigate."

"Our EVA's have GPS chips," Everett said. "They'll know right where to come."

"We appreciate the risk you're taking," Katla said.

The Kentuckian grinned. "All those days we spent cooped up in the tank, I'd like to think we became friends."

"Very much so," Trisna said, smiling at Pasco, who blushed.

At the next corner, they turned right. They were midway along the block when a Martian scrambled out from between two buildings and raised its eye stalks.

CHAPTER 21

"Only eighteen minutes until we're there," Major Howard announced from the pilot's seat.

"Only?" Kylo Carter said. "We can't get there fast enough to suit me."

"Makes two of us," Archard said. He was switching air canisters so his suit would have a fresh supply when they landed.

"Relax, you two," Major Howard said. "I'm in constant contact with Lieutenant Burroughs. She has patrols out, and there's no sign of the Martians."

"Let's hope it stays that way," the planetary scientist said.

Howard shifted in his seat. "What's gotten into you, sir? You're awful, I don't know, pessimistic all of a sudden."

"I'm worried, Major," Carter said. "Now that I've seen the Martians for myself, seen how formidable they are, I worry for the fate of Wellsville. Indeed, I worry for the fate of our colonization of Mars."

"If those things show their ugly faces in Wellsville, I'll have Burroughs fire up a RAM and Captain Rahn fire up his, and send out all three tanks," Major Howard said. "We'll show the Martians there's a new top dog on their planet."

"Your confidence overwhelms me, Major."

"They don't take wimps in the U.N.I.C.," Howard said. "Not in officer school. Weaklings are weeded out and only the toughest and the brightest graduate. Is that not so, Captain Rahn?"

"Not everyone can make it through the Academy, sir," Archard said diplomatically.

"There. You can quit your worrying, Mr. Carter," Major Howard said. "Wellsville isn't going to fall on my watch."

Archard recognized a disaster in the making when he saw one. Confidence was one thing, a zealot another. The major was blind to the reality of New Meridian. Worse, he underestimated the enemy, a critical mistake.

The planetary scientist turned and crooked a finger. "If you would, Captain."

Archard went over. "Sir?"

Lowering his voice so none of the others could hear, Carter said, "I need your best assessment. Will the colony still be there when we get back?"

"I'm guessing the Martians won't launch a full-scale attack until nightfall," Archard said. "They like the cover of darkness. Maybe it comes from living underground."

"On what do you base this assumption?"

"At New Meridian, they sent scouts into our tunnels and probed our defenses while the sun was up, but the main attack didn't come until after sunset."

"Hmm. Yes. I can see their logic. Darkness is their strength and our weakness. We don't see as well as they do. We can't fight as effectively. What else?"

"It's impossible to predict," Archard said. "They might do exactly as they did at New Meridian and try to overrun us by sheer force. Or they might not."

"I'm not a fan of ambiguity," Carter said. "Not with a colony at stake."

"It's the best I can do."

"I realize that," Carter said. "As intelligent as they must be, second guessing them won't be easy. But can you think of anything that might give us an edge?"

"The Martians don't have any weaknesses that I know of," Archard glumly acknowledged.

"Not one? Isn't there anything that struck you as bearing more investigation?"

"The thing that struck me the most about them was their headhunting," Archard said.

"I beg your pardon?"

"They took our heads. Everyone they killed, the heads were gone."

"Why didn't you tell me this sooner?"

"Is it important?"

"If they did it to everyone, most certainly. It must have special significance."

"Maybe they shrink the heads and save them," Archard joked.

"Something tells me there's more to it."

"Then you might like to know about the rest," Archard said. "What they do to the bodies."

"I was under the impression they rip the bodies to pieces."

"Yes and no," Archard said. "They tear off our arms and legs and set them on either side of our bodies, as neat as can be."

Carter rubbed his jaw in thought. "A ritual of some kind, possibly. And a ritual implies a religion."

Neither of them realized they were speaking loud enough to be overheard until Major Howard laughed.

"Did I hear you right, sir? The Martians have found God?" The major cackled.

"Nevertheless, it could be true," Carter said. "Most Earth civilizations have had religions, have they not?"

"I hope it is true," Major Howard surprised Archard by saying. "I hope they do believe in God. And in Hell. Especially Hell. Because that's where we're going to send every last one of those sons of bitches."

Katla froze in terror at the sight of the Martians. It was one of the small kind, incredibly fast and brutally savage. With her own eyes, she had seen them tear people limb from limb, seen them rip heads off.

Private Everett jerked his ICW to his shoulder, his finger curling to the trigger.

Suddenly, the creature whirled and darted back between the buildings.

"Stay here, ladies," Everett said. He made a hand signal to Private Pasco and the two warily advanced, their bodies slightly turned so that Everett covered to one side and Pasco to the other. Just short of the alley, both troopers faced into it so they were shoulder-to-shoulder. Another step, and they were there.

Katla braced for the blast of their weapons but they lowered their ICW's and looked at one another. "What is it?"

"The critter is gone," Private Everett said.

Katla and Trisna hurried up.

The alley wasn't more than two meters wide. Unlike olden days when alleys were littered with trash bins and garbage cans, this one was empty. No one threw refuse in a can anymore. That was what the Recycling Units were for.

"Where could it have gone?" Trisna anxiously asked.

"Beats me, lady," Everett said while scanning the walls and the rooftops.

"Why only the one?" Katla said.

"A scout, maybe," Everett said. "Getting the lay of the land."

"The lay of what?" Trisna said.

"An American and British expression," Private Pasco said. "Although the British use lie. It means to see how things are."

"Thank you," Trisna said softly.

Pasco blushed again.

"It's good news if we're right," Private Everett said. "If they're still scouting us out, they're not ready to attack. Gives us time to get you two to the Visitor Center."

They started off again, Piotr pressing his shoulder against Katla's leg. She smiled to reassure him, but it had no effect.

Not a single soul was abroad. Total silence had fallen, and with it a preternatural stillness. There wasn't even any wind, thanks to the domes.

As they came to the next intersection, Trisna unexpectedly stepped past Katla and up to Private Pasco. "Must you?" she said.

"Excuse me?" the young Spaniard replied.

"Must you drop us at the Visitor Center and go?" Trisna said.

"We must continue on patrol," Pasco said.

"Would you leave us to die, then?"

"Never," Pasco said.

"Yet that is what you will be doing. Without you to protect us, when the Martians attack, we will be defenseless. We will end up like all those good people in New Meridian. Our heads gone, our bodies in pieces." Pasco went to reply, but Trisna cut him off with, "You know I speak the truth. And I cannot believe you will abandon us to such a fate."

Swallowing, Pasco turned toward Everett.

"Don't even think it," the Kentuckian said.

"She's right. You can't deny that."

"Captain Rahn will be back soon. We'll tell him where the ladies are and he can handle things."

"What if the Martians attack before then?" Pasco argued. "Did we save these wonderful women in New Meridian only to have them be slaughtered here?"

"Damn you, you silly Spaniard," Everett said gruffly. "You like her, don't you? That's what this is about."

"I have said no such thing."

"You didn't have to, you ding-a-ling," Everett said. "If you were a buck, you'd be in rut right about now."

"I'd be in what?"

Katla was grinning, but her grin died when another pair of troopers came around a building farther down. One pointed, and they broke into a jog. "Uh-oh," she said.

Everett and Pasco stopped their squabbling and stepped in front of Katla and Trisna.

"Let us do the talking, ladies," the former said.

"I will not abandon them," Private Pasco said.

"You hush up, too," Everett said. "You'll give away how in love you are."

"I could just shoot you."

The other U.N.I.C. troopers weren't familiar to Katla. One was built like a proverbial tank and had corporal chevrons on his EVA suit. The other was a skin-and-bones private.

"Corporal Arnold. Private Niven," Private Everett greeted them. "How goes your patrol? We found a couple of ladies we're escorting to where they should be."

"They should have been off the streets long before this," Corporal Arnold said. "And what's with you two? Why did you turn your commlinks off?"

"We did?" Private Pasco said innocently.

"Don't play games, boy," Corporal Arnold growled.

"Lieutenant Burroughs has everyone out searching for you two."

"Oh, crap," Everett said.

"We can explain," Private Pasco said.

"Save it," Corporal Arnold said, and touched a gloved finger to the side of his helmet. "I just got word the major will be landing the Thunderbolt in a couple of minutes. You can explain to him."

"Double crap," Private Everett said.

Trisna Sahir was staring up through the dome at the

Martian sky. "I do not mean to worry anyone, but am I the only one who has noticed that the sun is setting?"

CHAPTER 22

Captain Archard Rahn stared out the viewport at the distant sun, about to slip beyond the rim of the Red Planet. Unlike Earth, where the sun was a vivid yellow, on Mars the thin atmosphere gave the illusion the sun was as white as ice. "The stars will be out soon."

The twin golden domes of Wellsville had swept into view and Major Howard was angling for a landing. "Strap yourselves in or hold tight. I'm going in fast and hard."

Archard was standing behind the seat Lydia Parkhill was in, firmly gripping the back. Even so, the deceleration nearly caused his legs to buckle.

The makeshift hangar was open to receive them.

Normally, a pilot would land outside and the aircraft would be wheeled in. But with time of the essence, Major Howard had radioed ahead to have the ground crew open the airlock so he could attempt a feat few pilots would dare. He descended until he was barely a meter above the ground, slowed until the Thunderbolt's lift was next to nil, and flew the aircraft in, coming to stop exactly in the middle.

"The proverbial dime," Kylo Carter said, and clapped in appreciation of the officer's feat.

"I was top in my class with a joystick," Major Howard boasted. "Simulators, jets, prop jobs, EmDrive, you name it, I could fly it."

"I believe you," Carter said.

Archard was impressed, too, but he didn't show it. The major was arrogant enough as it was.

The hanger door was slowly closing. Once it did, the air cycling system would kick in. That would take a while, though, and Archard was eager to leave. Donning his helmet, he sealed it and ran a systems check of his EVA suit that took all of twenty seconds. When his display showed green across the board, he made for the Thunderbolt's airlock.

"Hold on, Captain," Major Howard said. He had risen and was about to put his own helmet on. "Where do you think you're going?"

"To check on my friends," Archard said. He especially wanted to contact Katla.

"Personal matters will have to wait," Major Howard said. "You're under my orders now, and I need every trooper on active duty."

"Actually," Kylo Carter said as he unstrapped from his seat, "the captain has been assigned to me for the time being."

"What?" both Archard and Major Howard said at the same time.

"Check with Chief Administrator Reubens," Carter said.

"Unless a state of emergency has been imposed, he has the authority to override you."

"There better be a good reason," Major Howard said angrily.

"Captain Rahn has fought the Martians and lived to tell about it," Carter said. "His insights, his experience, are invaluable. The C.A. and I want him at our side so we can better direct affairs."

"*I'm* in command when it comes to military matters," Major Howard said. "The colonization protocols make that abundantly clear."

"And we wouldn't dream of interfering with you in the performance of your duties," Carter said. "You'll still have the rest of the troopers, including the two from New Meridian."

"Why wasn't I consulted first?"

"I'm doing so now. Surely you can see why it is imperative that we don't risk losing Captain Rahn in combat?"

Archard didn't care for the sound of that. "I'm a soldier. Protecting lives is what I do."

"I'm sorry, but Reubens and I have made up our minds," the planetary scientist said.

Major Howard scowled. "Go with him, then, Captain. You're to do as they say but stay in touch with me at all times. Understood?"

"Yes, sir," Archard said sullenly.

"Thank you for being so reasonable, Major," Kylo Carter said.

Containing his anger, Archard waited his turn at the airlock and went through with Sergeant Kline and Frank Parkhill. By then the hanger door had closed and the air had been recycled so that the farmer and his family didn't need EVA suits to reach the walkway to the dome.

Kline was tasked with ensuring the Parkhills were seen safely to the Visitor Center. He bobbed his helmet at Archard as they walked off.

"Now then," Kylo Carter said. "We're to proceed to the Administrative Center. From there, we'll oversee the colony's defenses."

"Wouldn't the Security Center be better?" Archard suggested.

"To what end? The troopers will be out and about, dealing with threats as they arise. We can advise them from Admin as well as we could from Security."

Archard tried a last gambit to get out of being taken from the fight. "I thought the major wanted me in my RAM to support the others?"

"Should it come to that, you will be." Carter smiled and clapped him on the back. "Cheer up. Look at the bright side. While your peers are engaging the Martians, you'll be snug and safe with Chief Administrator Reubens and me."

Archard could have punched him. "You don't understand the mentality of a warrior at all, do you?"

"Warriors have their uses, yes," Carter said. "And so do those of us who rely on our intellects more than our brawn." He gestured. "Now let's hurry. If your hunch is right, the Martians will make their move soon."

Katla was both relieved and disappointed. Relieved, in that Corporal Arnold had contacted his commanding officer and been told to escort her and Trisna to the Visitor Center. Disappointed, in that once they got there, Private Everett and Private Paso were to go with the corporal and Private Niven to conduct a sweep of the dome while other troopers swept the other one.

"You know," Katla said. "It isn't necessary for all four of you to take us. Private Everett and Private Pasco are more than enough."

Corporal Arnold shook his head. "The major said all four of us are to escort you and that's that."

"He tells you to jump and you ask how high?"

"That's how the military works, Doc," Arnold said. "Unlike civilians…" and he gave Katla and Trisna pointed glances…"we do as we're told."

"I've apologized for being out on the streets later than we should have," Katla said. "We've never been to Wellsville before. We got lost." She couldn't remember if that was the fifth or sixth lie she'd told since they got there.

"It happens," Corporal Arnold said.

Katla smiled her most winning smile and touched his arm.

"I don't suppose you could do me a favor?"

"Depends on what it is."

"Do you know Captain Rahn?"

"I met him when he arrived," Corporal Arnold said. "He looked pretty beat."

"Is it possible you could contact him on my behalf? I'd very much like to get word to him about where I am. Where we all are." Katla motioned at Piotr, Trisna, and Behula.

"I'm supposed to maintain radio silence unless it's important."

"I'd be very grateful."

Private Niven snickered. "Do you hear her, Corporal? Do you hear her trying to play you?"

"She's very good at it," Arnold said, and grinned at Katla.

"I'll tell you what, Doc. Since I don't want your captain mad at me, I'll get word to Lieutenant Burroughs when I can and ask her to relay your message. I'm not about to go through the major. He'd ream me a new one."

"Isn't that the truth," Private Niven said.

"Now quiet down, all of you," Corporal Arnold said. "We're supposed to be on the lookout for anything out of the ordinary."

"I still don't get why we have to wear these EVA suits," Private Niven said. "We're inside the dome, not outside."

Katla realized that neither Arnold nor Niven had been told about the Martians. Incredulous, she glanced over her shoulder at Everett and Pasco, who hadn't said a word in blocks. Neither said anything now.

Private Niven stopped dead and exclaimed, "What the hell was that?"

"What?" Corporal Arnold said.

"Something set off my motion sensor."

"What did?"

"I'm not sure."

Arnold was looking all around. "Where is it? Which direction?"

"I'm not sure of that, either. It was there and it was gone," Private Niven said.

"Your sensor is fritzing," Corporal Arnold said. "Nothing showed up on mine."

"Vishnu preserve us," Trisna said quietly.

"What was that?" Corporal Arnold said.

"I was praying."

Another block and a half, and they arrived at the Visitor Center. By then, darkness blanketed the domes, and lights had come on all over Wellsville.

"Allow me," Corporal Arnold said, holding the door for them.

"Don't forget you promised to get word to Captain Rahn," Katla reminded him.

"It's at the top of my to-do list," Arnold said.

"Please," she said.

"I told you I would and I will," Corporal Arnold said. "Now get in and stay put, ladies. If we run into you out here again, I won't be so nice." He smiled and shut the door.

"At least he did not arrest us," Trisna said.

Katla stood watching until the quartet reached the next corner. Corporal Arnold and Private Niven went one way, Private Everett and Private Pasco the other. Pasco looked back and started to give a little wave but Everett slapped his arm down.

"That Pasco is most adorable," Trisna said.

Katla had been wondering about something, and said, "You never did tell me what happened to your husband."

"He died in New Delhi shortly after Behula was born. He was in construction, and there was a mishap." Trisna cocked her head. "Why do you ask?"

"Just curious." Katla turned and made for the elevator.

"I wonder where Carla got to?" Trisna said. "No one is at the front desk."

"She could be anywhere," Katla said. "I just want to eat and lie down for a while."

Trisna laughed. "I forget we have our food in my handbag."

As the elevator rose, Piotr tiredly placed his cheek against Katla's leg and closed his eyes.

"Hang in there," Katla said.

Their rooms were 16 and 17 at the end of the hall. No sounds came from the other rooms they passed.

"There can't be very many people staying here, as quiet as it is," Trisna said.

Katla took out her key card and inserted it into the slot to 16. The light turned green and she worked the handle. A pungent odor assailed her, an all-too-familiar smell that caused a wave of horrific images from New Meridian to wash over her.

She turned on the light.

Piotr cried out.

Trisna turned Behula's face away.

For there, lying in a pool of blood, was a headless body. The arms and legs had been ripped off and placed to either side. Untouched by the blood, the nameplate on the blouse was easy to read.

Carla.

CHAPTER 23

The mantle of night cloaked the Red Planet when Captain Archard Rahn entered the Administrative Center with Planetary Scientist Kylo Carter.

The empty streets reminded Archard of New Meridian, of his attempt to keep the colonists safe by imposing a curfew, only to subsequently discover that sealing and locking doors and windows was no protection against creatures that attacked from below. Inadvertently, he'd turned every home in the colony into a death trap. The memory ate at him like acid.

Now, as an elevator whisked Carter and him to the top floor, Archard shifted his slung ICW from one shoulder to the other.

"I still think you should have left that EVA suit at the Security Center," Carter said. He had suggested as much earlier. "Why wear one when there is no need?"

"You never know," Archard said. "If the Martians breach the domes, I'll be glad I have it on."

"They didn't breach the domes at New Meridian, did they?"

"Not directly, no." Archard had given that a lot of thought. "They could have, any time they wanted. Which makes me think, as strange as this sounds, that they wanted to keep the colonists alive so they could kill everyone themselves."

"Are you implying they place a premium on personal combat? Like the Spartans of old?"

"I wouldn't know about that. All I'm saying is that they didn't attack our Atmosphere Center. Yet they have to be smart enough to know that if they did, it was all over for us."

"Interesting," the planetary scientist said.

A bell tinkled as the elevator opened and a simulated female voice announced, 'Fourth Floor. Executive Offices.'

"We're here," Carter needlessly said.

A plush hall brought them to wide oak double doors with brass fixtures and large brass letters that proclaimed *CHIEF ADMINISTRATOR*, and under that, *Evander Reubens*.

"Reminds me of politicians on Earth," Archard said.

"With their egos and their perks."

"Did you expect human nature to change simply because we're on a new planet?"

Simulated-wood paneling and a lush lavender carpet lent elegance to the reception area. A striking young woman sat at a desk working. When she looked up and saw who it was, she came to her feet.

"Mr. Carter! Chief Administrator Reubens is expecting you. He said you're to go right in."

"Thank you, Ms. Thern."

The C.A.'s office was fit for Earth royalty. It made C.A. Levlin Winslow's old office at New Meridian seem puny by comparison. Plush furniture, embossed curtains, a desk as long and wide as a bed, no expense had been spared to ensure that the chief administrator could perform his job in ease and luxury.

Reubens was at his desk, involved in a call with someone. He wasn't alone. Four civil servant types were in chairs facing him. All four rose to greet Carter and shake his hand, and then waited for Reubens to get done.

Archard hung back. It struck him as the height of insanity to indulge in all this petty formality when the welfare of the colony hung in the balance.

At last, Reubens ended his call and sat up. "Kylo! You're here at last. And you've brought Captain Rahn."

"Per your request, so we have access to his expertise," Carter said.

"I have to tell you," Reubens said, stretching. "I'm beginning to think it's a false alarm. The Martians attacked the agrifarms, yes, but there's been precious little sign of them here. Major Howard is at the Security Center with Lieutenant Burroughs and Sergeant Kline. They're monitoring every camera in the colony, and so far there hasn't been any sign of any Martians. We also have three patrols out, and not one has reported a sighting."

Archard felt compelled to ask, "Are Privates Everett and Pasco on those patrols?"

"They're paired up, yes, I do believe," Reubens said. "As are Corporal Arnold with Private Nivens, and Private Bova with Private Heinlein."

Those last names meant nothing to Archard. He hadn't met them yet.

"The captain was certain the Martians would attack once the sun went down," Carter mentioned.

Reubens gestured at a window, at the dome and the stars visible through it. "If that's the case, they're taking their sweet time about it."

"If you ask me," a heavyset assistant said, "this is another instance of the military crying wolf. They like to puff out their chests now and then to remind everyone of how important they are." He smiled at Archard. "No offense meant."

"None taken," Archard lied.

The intercom buzzed, and Reubens pressed a button. "Yes?"

"Sir," the receptionist said. "There's a woman on line six. She says her name is Dr. Katla Dkany, and that you know her, and that she needs to speak to you right away."

Archard took a half-step toward the desk.

Reubens pressed another button above a blinking light. "Dr. Dkany? How good to hear from you again. How may I be of help?"

"We're at the Visitor Center…" Katla started to say, the speaker making her voice sound tinny.

"We?" Reubens interrupted.

"Trisna Sahir and her daughter and Piotr Zabinski and me."

Archard could tell that Katla was upset and trying not to show it. He took another step.

"Yes, I authorized the vouchers for all of you to stay there, remember?" Reubens was saying.

"I called to warn you that the Martians are in Wellsville."

"My dear woman," Reubens said patronizingly. "There hasn't been a sign of them anywhere."

"Then you haven't looked in the Visitor Center," Katla said. "They're here, and they're killing people."

Katla had more to say but the line went dead. She tried to get a dial tone but all she heard was a hum.

"Please, let us leave," Trisna said from the doorway to the room. She had Behula in one arm and was holding Piotr's hand. Glancing at the ghastly remains on the floor, she shuddered. "We should have gone the second we saw her."

"The C.A. needed to know," Katla said. "So they can warn everyone."

"I don't hear sirens," Trisna said.

"Give it time." Katla sidled around the body, careful not to step in the blood. Piotr let go of Trisna to dash to her and clutch her hand. Katla was almost to the hall when she stopped and looked back.

"What?" Trisna said.

"There's no hole in the floor. At New Meridian, the Martians always came up through the floors."

"We are not at ground level," Trisna said. "We're on the second story."

"Even so," Katla said. "Where did the Martian come from? Where did it get to?"

Trisna flinched as if she'd been slapped. She fearfully looked down the hallway, then at the walls and the ceiling. "It could be anywhere. They cling to things like flies."

Treading lightly, they started back down the hall. At the next room, Katla stopped again. Putting a finger to her lips, she pressed an ear to the door. She heard nothing. She tried the handle, but without the proper key card, she couldn't open it.

"What are you doing?" Trisna whispered.

"There might be others like Carla."

"We can do them no good on our own," Trisna said. "We need soldiers." She paused. "And I still do not hear sirens."

"Let's go, then."

"Thank Vishnu," Trisna said.

The elevator was still on their floor. Katla pressed the down button and when the doors slid open, she cautiously checked inside. No Martians.

Trisna moved to a corner. "This might have been a trap. They let us come up so they could cut us off, and they'll be waiting below."

"We only saw the one out in the street," Karla said as the doors closed.

"Where there is one, there are hundreds. You know that as well as I."

The elevator braked, and Karla tensed. If Trisna was right, they would be swarmed the moment the doors opened.

"Katla?" Piotr said in dismay. "What do we do?"

"Be strong."

The doors hissed, revealing an empty lobby.

Katla pulled Piotr toward the entrance. She figured to head for U.N.I.C. headquarters. That was where she would probably find Archard. It also promised to be the safest place in Wellsville, what with the troopers and their armaments.

"I hate this," Trisna whispered. "It reminds me too much of before."

Katla felt Piotr's hand tremble. "It's not that bad."

"Yet," Trisna said.

With the stars out, the shadows had lengthened. The empty streets and the eerie silence compounded Katla's unease. She had been incredibly lucky to survive the attack on New Meridian. She might not be so lucky this time.

Staying close to the buildings, she proceeded at a slow clip. There was no sense in running with everyone so tired, and eight or nine blocks to travel.

Trisna practically trod on her heels. When Katla thought she heard a sound and stopped, Trisna bumped into her.

"A little space, if you don't mind."

"I am sorry. I'm scared."

Katla listened, but the sound wasn't repeated. She continued on. Perhaps, she told herself, there were only a few Martians. Otherwise, she would be hearing screams and wails and the din of widespread destruction.

Behind her, Trisna gasped.

Katla glanced back. "What is it now?"

Trisna pointed at the rooftop across the street.

At first, Katla didn't realize what she was seeing. Decorative protrusions on the coping, she assumed. Then a pair of the protrusions moved, swaying from side to side, and her blood turned to ice as it dawned on her that they were eyes. Lots and lots of Martian eyes. Peering over the roof, at them.

"We are dead," Trisna said.

CHAPTER 24

Levlin Winslow had never been so excited in his life. As he scrabbled from the huge cavern with Nilista at his side, the irony didn't elude him. The two of them were part of a great swarm of Martians flowing up through a network of tunnels toward the underside of Wellsville, intent on ripping apart beings from his former homeworld and turning them into creatures just like him.

Winslow had no reservations whatsoever. He liked his new form, his new body, and his newfound mental abilities. Or sentient abilities, as the Martians would describe them. He was more alive than he had ever been, more aware of himself and everything around him.

"*You are happy, my bindmate,*" Nilista's consciousness flowed into his.

"*Never more so,*" Winslow admitted.

"*Your conversion to the Unity has gone well. On rare occasions, they do not. I am glad you have not had any difficulties.*"

Winslow's senses registered the dimensions of the tunnel and the presence of the other Martians without him having to think about it. The tunnel was new, dug by giant drillers for the attack on the colony. "*What kind of difficulties?*"

"*Some are unable to join their sentience to the Unity,*" Nilista said. "*Others go mad.*"

"*What happens to them?*"

"*Those who cannot achieve Unity are spared further aloneness by being reduced to their component elements.*"

"*They are killed?*"

"*They are destroyed, yes,*" Nilista said. "*What else is there to do for them? Those who exist outside the Unity are particles of emptiness who contribute nothing of worth to the Source of All. So their sentience is extracted and returned to the Oversoul.*"

"*The what?*" It was the first time Winslow had heard the term.

"*I will educate you on the Oversoul later, after we have converted the Blue Worlders above us. In the meantime, you might work on yet another aspect of your conversion.*"

"*Which is?*"

"*When our conscious selves merge, I can sense that you still refer to yourself with your former name. You are one of us now. One of the Unity. You should use your Unity name.*"

"*I didn't know I had one.*"

"*You are known by us as Kralun. Unlike Blue World names, which have simple meanings, our names are compounded of deeper significance. Yours means relishes-eager-overcomes.*"

Winslow rolled his new name on his mental tongue, enjoying the soundless sound of it. "*Kralun,*" he repeated. "*I like it.*"

"*You are it and it is you. Be it. Think it. Let the name Winslow be of the past. A memory that will fade until there is only Kralun.*"

"*I see the wisdom of that,*" Winslow thought, and corrected himself with, *Kralun sees the wisdom, Kralun sees the wisdom, Kralun sees the wisdom.*

"*I am proud of you, bindmate.*"

"*And I am grateful that you are. You do me great honor, Nilista.*"

"*When I first touched your mind, I liked the taste of you. I sensed your potential. Sensed that you and I could enjoy the deep and full rapture of being one.*"

"*I have never known such joy as I did when we joined bodies.*"

"*You will experience that joy many times in our long lives together.*"

"*I have died and gone to heaven.*"

"*The context is new to me.*"

"*It is an expression from the Blue World.*"

"*That life is dead to you. Immerse yourself in the new and let the old pass away.*"

"*Yes, I will.*"

"*And remember,*" Nilista said. "*Once we leave these tunnels, we must use the utmost stealth. The Hryghr would have us fill every shadow with our numbers, and at their signal, rush out together. It will be over before the Blue Worlders can fight back, and we will lose but few."*

"I hope it works."

"How can it not? We are of the Unity and in the Unity, and the Unity always prevails. Rest secure in that knowledge, Kralun."

"Yes," Kralun said. *"I will."*

The terror in Piotr Zabinski's eyes spurred Katla into scooping him into her arms and saying, "Run!" She took her own advice and sprinted toward the next corner. Any moment, she expected the creatures to pour down the side of the building and overwhelm them.

Behind her, Trisna huffed and puffed.

Katla did some puffing of her own. Piotr wasn't light, somewhere between sixty and seventy pounds. She would rather put him down and have him run on his own but he was frozen in fear.

"Why are they not after us?" Trisna said.

Katla reached the junction and stopped to look back. The Martians were still up there, their eyes swaying and bobbing as they always did. But the creatures hadn't given chase.

"I do not understand," Trisna said.

"Keep running!" Katla urged. She turned to continuing fleeing and collided with someone coming the other way. Stumbling, she dropped Piotr, who managed to land on his feet. She was appalled to realize she had collided with a trooper and blurted, "Please don't arrest us! We have a reason for being outside!"

"Relax, Doc. It's only Pasco and me," Private Everett said, cradling his weapon.

The young Spaniard smiled, his eyes drinking in Trisna. "We were worried about you so we went around the block and came back. The corporal would have a fit if he knew."

"You ladies should have stayed in the Visitor Center," Private Everett said. "Didn't you learn anything earlier?"

"No! Stop!" Katla finally got a word in edgewise. Grabbing the Kentuckian by the shoulders, she pointed at the rooftops on the other side of the street. "Haven't you seen them?"

"What are you…?" Everett began, and went rigid with alarm.

"Madre de Dios, can it be?" Pasco said.

"We found a dead body in the Visitor Center," Trisna told him. "The woman who ran it. They tore her arms and legs off and took her head, as they did to everyone at New Meridian."

"Not again," Pasco said.

Everett moved around Katla and Trisna, putting himself between them and the Martians. "Keep going. We have to find somewhere safe and I'll call this in."

"Shouldn't you call it in first?" Katla said.

"They might order us to engage the critters and leave you on your own," Everett said. "You want that?"

No, Katla didn't. Unarmed, she and Trisna stood no prayer whatsoever. "The only safe place is your headquarters."

"We can't go there, Dr. Dkany," Private Pasco said. "They would put all of us in cells. Everett and me for dereliction of duty, and Trisna and you for violating the curfew."

"But if we explain about the Martians?" Trisna said.

"It won't do any good unless they see the creatures for themselves," Private Everett said. "Now enough jabber. We have to hunt cover, and pronto. Those things won't stay up yonder forever."

Katla didn't need urging. To stay in the open invited being ripped to pieces. Gripping Piotr's hand, she jogged with the rest.

"Is there somewhere you can think of, Private Pasco?" Trisna asked.

Pasco shook his helmet. "We are not familiar with Wellsville yet."

"And we may never get to be," Everett said.

Katla wished he would use more discretion. She gave Piotr a reassuring squeeze but once again he had gone deep into himself, the only place he was safe from the terrors of the outside world.

Katla went past a short flight of stairs that led down to a darkened doorway but stopped when Private Everett said her name.

Above a closed retractable metal door to a long single-story building hung a sign that read *Wellsville Warehouse #2.*

As required by the colonization protocols, every colony maintained a stock of emergency supplies and parts in designated warehouses. New Meridian, with its smaller population and single dome, only had one warehouse. Wellsville had two.

"That door would slow our tank," Private Everett remarked.

"It would slow the Martians, too, I bet," Private Pasco said.

"We'll stash you here, Doc," Everett said, "and get word to the captain."

"I don't know," Katla said.

"The warehouses are reinforced," Private Everett informed her. "In case of quakes and whatnot." Without waiting for her to approve, he went down the steps, took out a U.N.I. C. key card, and swiped it.

"I do not want to be separated from you again," Trisna said to Pasco.

From within the warehouse sounded a series of loud clicks followed by the muted rumble of large gears. The metal door began to rise.

Everett turned toward Trisna and her daughter. "You're better off here than anywhere else, ma'am. Trust us."

Katla was about to point out that trust wasn't the issue when a pair of multifaceted eyes poked from under the rising door, and an instant later, a pair of pincers.

They were reaching for Everett.

"Behind you!" Katla yelled.

The Kentuckian spun, leveling his ICW as he turned. He appeared about to fire but didn't when the creature scuttled back out of sight.

The door continued to rise. Lights were supposed to come on automatically, but the interior was as black as the bottom of a well.

Private Pasco darted down next to Everett and switched on his EVA suit's helmet lamp. The bright beam lit up the expansive interior, bathing crates and containers and boxes and pallets. It also revealed a multitude of Martians clinging to every centimeter of available space. The floor, the walls, the ceiling, the creatures were everywhere.

Katla broke out in gooseflesh.

CHAPTER 25

Captain Archard Rahn had long taken pride in his devotion to duty. He was a career soldier, a model trooper who always followed orders to the T. Anything and everything the United Nations Interplanetary Command had ever demanded of him, he did. It was a large part of why he was one of the few chosen for Mars. The list of applicants was thousands long, but the U.N.I.C. only sent their best when it came to their officers.

Never in a million years would Archard have considered disobeying an order. Never, ever, would he have imagined putting anyone or anything before the U.N.I.C.

That was before New Meridian. Before the stunning revelations the planetary scientist shared. The worst of it, the very worst as far as Archard was concerned, was that the chief administrators and the governor and Archard's own commanding officers had conspired to leave the third colony hanging in the Martian wind when the Martians attacked.

It was a severe blow to Archard's psyche. An integral aspect to military service was trust. Soldiers not only had to know they could trust their buddies in the heat of combat, they had to know they could trust their superiors to not put them in harm's way unless it was absolutely necessary.

The United Nations Interplanetary Command and the Earth governments that sponsored and supported it, had betrayed Archard's trust. His, and the entire populations of first New Meridian and now Wellsville. Those who were supposed to put the safety of the lives under them before all else had done nothing while those lives were being snuffed.

Archard simmered with rage at the injustice of it. The deception was sheer evil. He no longer trusted those in authority. Not Chief Administrator Reubens, not Kylo Carter, not Major Howard. Not the governor or the commander at Bradbury, either.

So now, as he stood listening to Reubens and Carter debate what to do over a holo link with Major Howard at the Security Center, Archard made up his own mind.

"I can send troopers to the Visitor Center to extract the doctor and her friend," Major Howard was saying. "Corporal Arnold and Private Niven are only a few blocks away. The two new recruits from New Meridian are supposed to be in the area, too, but I've lost contact with them. Either they've turned off their commlinks or…"

"Or the Martians have killed them," Kylo Carter said.

"Which makes extracting the women problematic," Chief Administrator Reubens said. "The remaining troopers are more important. We might want to pull Arnold and Niven out of there."

"And leave the women on their own?" Carter said.

"For the greater good of the colony, yes," Chief Administrator Reubens said.

"I agree," Major Howard said. "If this is a full-scale attack, I need every soldier we have."

Archard was filled with disgust for all three of them. Turning, he made for the door, unslinging his ICW as he went.

"Hold on there, Captain," Kylo Carter said. "Where are you going?"

"You know where," Archard said.

The holo image of Major Howard thrust a finger at him. "I've given no such order. You will stand down and remain where you are."

"Like hell," Archard said.

Kylo Carter came toward him. "I understand. They're from New Meridian. You feel obligated."

"New Meridian is gone," Reubens said coldly. "Wellsville is all that matters now."

"Not for me," Archard said.

Major Howard's holo raised its voice. "This is a direct command, Captain. You are not to leave this room. Understood?"

"Get stuffed, sir."

Howard's holo shook a fist. "You've just ended your career, mister. You hear me? I will have you thrown in the guardhouse and brought up on charges."

"Before or after the Martians overrun us?" Archard said. He reached the door, and looked back. "If you want my advice, Major, you'll get a trooper in your RAM and send others out in the tanks. This colony is about to become a killing field."

"Captain Rahn, please," Kylo Carter said. "You're letting your emotions get the better of you."

"Damn straight I am."

"How very foolish," Chief Administrator Reubens said.

"Two women and two children need our help, and you three throw them to the wolves without batting an eye," Archard said. "I'd rather be a fool than what you are."

"I'll send troopers to place you under arrest," Major Howard warned.

"With the Martians about to attack?" Archard scoffed. "Like you said, you need every soldier for the battle ahead."

"There might not even be one," Reubens said. "For all we know, the Martians are only scouting us out. Isn't that how you military types describe it?"

"You're a bigger jackass than I thought," Archard said. He opened the door.

"One last chance," Major Howard called out. "Stand down this instant."

"Not going to happen, sir," Archard said.

"If I have any say," Major Howard said, "it will be a firing squad for you."

"If you're still breathing after the Martians get done, come see me," Archard said. Stepping out, he hurried to the elevator. He half-expected to find troopers in the lobby but there were only civilians who stared, mystified, as he sprinted to the outer doors, used his U.N.I.C. override card to open them, and burst out into the Martian night.

Archard keyed his commlink. He knew that the major and every other trooper using the military frequency would hear him, but he didn't care. "Private Everett. Private Pasco. This is Captain Rahn. Report your positions."

His earphones hissed with static.

"Privates Everett, Pasco. Report in, please," Archard tried a second time.

Again, they failed to respond.

Archard ran faster. Either they had turned off their commlinks---or they really were dead. At the next intersection, he turned left onto a side street and was halfway along it when he happened to glance up at the buildings on either side. They were shrouded in darkness. He switched on his night vision and was jarred to his marrow.

The top levels of all the buildings were covered with Martians. Hanging by their eight legs, the creatures were perfectly still except for the swaying of their eye stalks.

Archard's first impulse was to open fire. It would be his last if he did. Hurrying on, he resorted to his commlink again. "Major Howard, do you read me?"

The hissing continued.

"Major Howard, I have critical intel. Answer me for your own good."

The major didn't reply.

It was amazing, Archard reflected, how childish some people could be.

"This is Lieutenant Burroughs," a crisp female voice declared. "I read you, Captain. What is the nature of your intel?"

Before Archard could reply, Major Howard broke his silence.

"This is the Major, Lieutenant Burroughs. You will disregard Captain Rahn, and anything he has to say."

"Major?" Burroughs said uncertainly.

"Lieutenant, listen to me," Archard said quickly. "I'm on Sturgeon Street. Martians are all over the place. They're massed, but they haven't attacked yet."

Burroughs started to say something but Major

Howard overrode her. "Our sensors don't show any such infestation. You will disregard his claim, Lieutenant."

"Sir?" Burroughs said.

Archard gave it one last try with, "Burroughs, if you care about the people in this colony, you'll gear up. The war has come to your door, and your commanding officer is too stupid to see it."

Major Howard began swearing.

Archard cut the connection and ran. He had blocks to cover. Katla, he thought, here I come.

Above him, on both sides of the street, the Red Planet's indigenous life stared and did nothing. As if they were waiting.

But for what?

Katla Dkany became ice cold with fear. There were so many creatures lurking in the warehouse that she and those with her could overwhelmed in heartbeats. "Back away," she said quietly. "Back away quickly."

Private Everett nodded, hesitated, then pressed the control for the door and retreated up the stairs. Pasco hastily followed suit.

The door was descending, and making a lot of noise.

Inside, the Martians didn't move except for their always-in-motion eyes.

Trisna was mouthing a prayer under her breath.

"Katla?" Piotr said anxiously.

"Shhhh," Katla said, and gently squeezed his arm. "They're not coming after us. Stay calm." Which was easy for her to say. Her stomach was a fluttery mess and her pulse was racing.

Everett and Pasco kept their weapons trained on the warehouse until the door came to rest with a thud.

"What do we do? What do we do?" Pasco said. "This is bad, bad, bad."

"We have to let the bigwigs know," Everett said.

"They'll be able to get a fix on our location," Pasco said, and gave Trisna and Katla meaningful looks.

"Can't be helped," Everett said. "It's the whole colony now, not just us."

"Do it," Katla said.

"Yes," Trisna agreed.

"Switching on my commlink," Private Everett said, and then, in a more formal tone, "Patrol Able to Command. Patrol Able to Command. Do you read me? Over?" He tilted his helmet as if listening, and his brow puckered. "Hold on. Three of you are talking at once. Everything is garbled. Captain Rahn? Is that you?" He listened some more, and said, "Switching to designated frequency."

"What's going on?" Private Pasco said.

Everett motioned for silence, then listened and nodded a few times. "Yes, sir. I know where that is. We'll have them there in five. Roger. Out."

"Don't keep us in suspense," Katla said.

"The Martians are all over," Everett said. "Captain Rahn is on his way. We're to rendezvous with him about two blocks from here, on Gaskell Street."

"Reunite with the captain," Trisna said. "That is good."

"On me," Everett said, and assumed the lead. "Pasco, cover our butts."

"*Si.*"

"What was that about garbled?" Katla was curious to learn.

"Major Howard and Lieutenant Burroughs jumped on about the same time," Everett explained. "The major wanted Pasco and me to report to the Security Center, ASAP. Then the captain told me to switch frequencies, and here we are."

"I can't wait to see him," Katla said without thinking.

"I'm shocked, ma'am," Everett said.

Pasco chuckled and Trisna grinned.

Katla was amazed that anyone could crack jokes or even laugh at a time like this. She craned her neck, scanning the tops of the buildings. Sure enough, more creatures were up there. A terrible lot of them.

"If anyone can see us to safety, it is the captain," Trisna said. "I have complete confidence in him."

"You and me both, lady," Private Everett said. "Which is why I'm doing what he wants and not what the major said to do."

"Major Howard will punish us when this is over," Private Pasco predicted.

"If we're all still alive, he's welcome to," Everett said.

Katla had to force herself to stop staring at the rooftops. She concentrated on Piotr, on keeping him close.

High above the dome, stars sparkled, casting their indifferent light over the bloodbath soon to occur.

"I just realized," Trisna said. "The people in their homes and businesses. They have no idea the colony is being invaded."

"Thanks to the C.A. and his phony gas leak," Everett said. "I hope the critters rip him into itty-bitty bits."

"Why does the captain wants us to meet him on Gaskell Street?" Pasco said. "Why not headquarters?"

"Ask him when we see him."

Katla listened with half an ear. She was probing every shadow, every unlit nook and cranny. When the assault came, it would be swift and brutal.

"I wish I was back on Earth," Trisna said. "I wish I never came to Mars."

"Hindsight is great for blaming ourselves," Katla said. Not that she would ever regret coming. It was the great adventure of her life. Martians or not.

The buildings they passed were an eclectic mix of architectural modules to fit the many nationalities involved. The psych experts claimed that constructing a colony as Earth-like as possible enabled the colonists to acclimate more fully. Home away from home, was the ages-old motto. Evidently, it applied to planets, too.

Across the way was a structure fashioned like those in Paris, closer stood another that resembled a house in Thailand, and yet again a building that gave the illusion of being transplanted from Europe.

The Martians showed no preference. They clung to everything.

They came to Gaskell Street and stopped next to an old-style market. It had sliding doors and a glass front, and was closed.

"Where can the captain be?" Private Pasco said.

Katla was wondering the same thing when a helmet light flared inside and Archard opened the door to admit them. Entering, she threw both arms around him and whispered, "I've missed you."

To her surprise, Archard pulled back. "You're not wearing an EVA suit." He looked past her at Trisna.

"Neither of you. Or the kids."

"We have not had cause to put one on," Trisna said as she moved to checkout and wearily leaned against it. Behula had fallen asleep and stirred but didn't awaken.

"And it's not as if we can buy one in a clothes shop," Katla said, miffed that he had ignored her outpouring of affection.

"We have to find you EVA's," Archard said. "In case of a breach."

"Sir, look!" Private Everett broke in, and pointed.

A pair of troopers in full gear were jogging up the street toward the market.

"It must Corporal Arnold and Private Niven," Private Pasco said. "They were in the area."

"I'll handle this," Archard said, and stood in the doorway, blocking entry. "Gentlemen," he called out.

"What can I do for you?"

Peering through the tinted window, Katla saw the pair separate, as if they anticipated trouble.

"Captain Rahn, sir," Corporal Arnold said. "Major Howard sent us to fetch you and these others back to the Security Center."

"I'm afraid we can't accommodate the major," Archard said.

"He was quite specific, sir," Corporal Arnold said. "We're not to take no for an answer."

"No," Archard said.

Private Everett and Private Pasco took flanking positions on either side of him.

"Please don't make this any harder than it has to be," the corporal said.

"That's up to you," Archard said.

"Sir, what is this about?" Corporal Arnold said. "How can you disobey a direct order?"

"Haven't you seen the Martians?"

"Of course. Which is why we have to hurry. Please, sir."

Katla could tell Archard was reluctant to force the issue. The next moment, the matter was taken out of his hands by a low thrumming sound the likes of which she had never heard before. A sound that penetrated her body, somehow, and caused every bone in her skeleton to vibrate like the tines on a turning fork.

Behula, snapping awake, screamed.

Piotr cried out.

The thrum lasted a good fifteen seconds, then faded.

"What in creation was that?" Private Everett said.

"It rattled me good."

Corporal Arnold was tapping the side of his helmet. "I've lost contact with the major."

In the sudden silence, another strange sound fell on their ears. This time, it was a scritching and scratching, as if a thousand cats were running their claws over stone.

"The Martians!" the corporal cried.

Katla saw them, too.

A living tide of eyes and limbs and grippers streamed from the adjacent rooftops.

CHAPTER 26

Captain Archard Rahn's worst dread had come to pass. He'd hoped to whisk Katla and Trisna Sahir to U.N.I.C. and fit them with EVA suits before the attack began.

Raising his ICW, Archard yelled, "Everett! Pasco! On me! Arnold, Niven, protect the women!"

The Kentuckian and the Spaniard were quick to comply. Archard barely had time to bark, "Back to back, in a circle."

Then the creatures were on them.

Flipping the ICW's selector to full auto, Archard brought down the first rank of scuttling crustoids. He heard the others fire, saw creatures falling right and left. There were so many that for a harrowing half-a-minute, he was sure he and the rest would be buried in an avalanche of horrors. But their circle held, and scores of the things lay thrashing and kicking when those behind slowed.

"Incendiaries!" Archard bellowed, and let fly.

A blast of chemical fire engulfed a dozen creatures, frying them in their carapaces. Their eyes melted, their eye stalks oozed like wax.

All around, Martians died in flames, expanding the space between the troopers and their adversaries.

"Frags!" Archard roared, and flicked his selector. "Range, twenty-five meters." He was cutting it close. The kill radius was fifteen. That gave them a safety margin of ten, but sometimes fragments were propelled further than fifteen.

The microchips that controlled their ICW's functions performed flawlessly. A series of explosions, one after the other, went off exactly twenty-five meters out. Creatures were obliterated. Huge numbers of others were wounded and crippled.

Archard was mildly surprised to see the inhuman phalanx brought to a stop. There weren't as many as he had thought. Then again, the roofs could only hold limited numbers. "Semi-auto!" he shouted, and began dropping Martians as fast as he could aim and squeeze the trigger.

In well-trained synchrony, he and the rest of the troopers unleashed a hailstorm, overlaying their fields of fire for maximum effect. In less time than Archard would have thought possible, every Martian in the street was either dead or dying.

"Cease fire!" Archard bawled. In the quiet that ensued, his ears rang. His helmet had dampened the noise of the blasts and the autofire, but not entirely. He heard Private Pasco whoop.

A sound from far off prompted Archard to boost the volume. The night came alive with a cacophony of death; explosions, screams, shots, shrieks and wails and pleas for help. The Martians were attacking all over.

"Reload," Archard said, in case any of the others had neglected to do so in the excitement. He ejected his magazine and slapped in another. "Katla! Trisna!" he said through his external mic. "We have to go. Now."

The women cautiously emerged from the market, Katla holding Piotr's hand, Trisna cradling her daughter.

"Where to?" Katla said.

"U.N.I.C. headquarters," Archard said. "Their armaments are our only chance of staying alive." He faced the troopers. "Everett, Pasco, you're with us. Corporal Arnold, Private Niven, do as you want. I won't order you to defy your major."

The corporal seemed stunned by the onslaught. He gazed out over the carnage as a sheet of flame erupted from a building blocks away. "Do you see that? Do you hear that? Why didn't they warn us something like this could happen?"

"Major! Major!" Private Niven tried his commlink. "Do you copy? Over."

"Good luck, you two," Archard said. "The rest of you, move to the middle of the street." He signaled, and Private Everett took point. Pasco would automatically bring up the rear, placing the women and children between them.

"Wait, sir," Corporal Arnold said, turning. "We'll go with you."

"We will?" Private Niven said.

"We're cut off from command," Corporal Arnold said. "On our own. With the colony under attack by a horde of those things, I say we stick with the captain. Otherwise, how long will we last?"

Niven raised his faceplate to the sheet of flame in the distance, and to another that had flared to the south. He shook his head. "I'm with you, Arnie. We'll stay with these guys. We're U.N.I.C. Booyah!"

Arnold, Everett, and Pasco all echoed him in unison with a "Booyah!" of their own.

"In that case," Archard said, "Arnold and Niven, you're flankers. Arnold right, Niven left. Don't let anything reach the women or the kids."

"Yes, sir," both responded.

Twenty meters out, Private Everett was like a cougar on the prowl, swinging from side to side, his ICW wedged to his shoulder.

Archard pegged his sensors at max. His helmet display, while not as sophisticated as that in the RAM 3000, showed no heat signatures in the windows of the buildings, nor any hint of movement on the rooftops. But from all over the colony, the cries of colonists being attacked rose intermittently, punctuated by occasional autofire and twice by grenade blasts. Not long after that he heard the unmistakable boom of a tank cannon.

Archard switched to the U.N.I.C. command frequency. Major Howard was bellowing orders. A tank had been dispatched with Privates Heinlein and Bova, and the major was telling Sergeant Kline to bring a second tank to the Administrative Center and pick him up.

Then Howard said, "Lieutenant Burroughs, are you suited up yet?"

"Almost ready, sir," was her reply.

"You should have engaged the enemy five minutes ago."

"It takes longer to prep a RAM when you're doing it yourself," Burroughs said, adding almost as an afterthought, "sir."

"It should have already been prepped, Lieutenant," Major Howard snapped. "I don't accept excuses. I only accept results."

"Yes, sir."

"That battle suit is our best hope of protecting this colony," Howard said. "If that damn Rahn hadn't gone off on his own, I'd have him gear up in the suit he brought from New Meridian. Between the two of you, we'd contain these Martians."

Archard had his doubts. The RAM 3000's were the most lethal killing machines ever made, yes, but the Martians had a near-insurmountable advantage in sheer numbers.

Archard clicked his mic. "This is Captain Rahn. We are en route to the Security Center. Once we get there, I will outfit the second RAM and coordinate with Lieutenant Burroughs."

"Well, well, well," Major Howard said sarcastically. "Trying to make amends for your insubordination?"

"I won't have a second colony go down around me," Archard said. Not if he could help it.

"ETA to SC?" Lieutenant Burroughs asked.

Archard consulted his readout. "Eight minutes. We're on foot and there are Martians everywhere."

"Who is this 'we' you keep referring to?" Major Howard said.

Archard rattled off the names of the four troopers. "We're escorting Dr. Katla Dkany, Trisna Sahir and her daughter, and the Zabinski boy."

"Five soldiers to safeguard four civilians?" Major Howard said. "That's what I call a reckless waste of manpower. But very well. Corporal Arnold, do you read me?"

"Yes, sir," Arnold joined in.

"When you arrive at headquarters, I want you and Niven to man the third tank and hustle to the other dome."

"Will do, sir."

"And Captain Rahn?"

"Sir?" Archard said.

"For the time being, I will let things ride. The crisis takes precedence. But once this is over, once we've repelled these things and resorted order, I intend to bring you up on charges.

Are we clear?"

Lieutenant Burroughs cut in with, "Captain Rahn? I've fired up the RAM, and I'm running a last systems check. Any advice you can give me? You've fought these creatures. I haven't."

"Airborne is your best bet," Archard instructed her. "Keep your distance and use your arsenal as needed. Don't engage the blue ones hand-to-hand if you can help it. They can rip right through your suit."

"The devil you say," Burroughs said. "These babies are supposed to be impenetrable."

"Tell that the Martians," Archard said. "And watch out for the Flyers. If there are enough of them, then can bring you down."

"Wait. Some of the Martians can fly? Why hasn't anyone told us all of this?"

"Ask your major," Archard said.

"Enough chatter," Major Howard said. "Lieutenant, get your ass out there. Rahn, get yours to headquarters and suit up to help her. And pray our hardware saves the day."

Amen to that, Archard thought.

Levlin Winslow clung to the side of a building in his new form and tingled with expectation. The gathering would commence any moment

All around were other Gryghr. Nilista was at his side, her consciousness entwined with his. She was excited, too.

Winslow was trying to only think of himself as Kralun the Martian but old mental habits were hard to break. *I am Kralun. I am Kralun. I am Kralun*, he said over and over to drum it into himself.

"*The call will come soon,*" Nilista said. "*Merge in the Unity.*"

Concentrating, Winslow experienced his awareness slipping into the communal stream. A confusing jumble of images and sights tumbled through him. He was one with the host, and almost lost in it. When the eye stalks of those nearest him turned, his turned his, too. Some sort of synchronous movement on a subliminal level, he figured.

Winslow focused, and the stream became clearer. He was aware of his distinct sentience and yet simultaneously aware of being merged with the others. It was unsettling.

I am Kralun, he thought. *I can do this.*

"*You can do this,*" Nilista assured him.

Winslow wished the two of them could go off alone and bind again.

"*Be ready. The call is upon us.*"

Winslow was going to ask what form the call would take when it happened. He and every other Martian stiffened as their carapaces, indeed, their entire bodies, were permeated by a vibratory sensation that heightened their senses to their utmost. It was like jumping into an ice-cold lake or being jolted by a bolt of lightning.

As one, the Gryghr flowed down the wall to the street. Winslow was aware of moving yet not aware that he was consciously doing so. He was the Unity and the Unity was him.

Ahead loomed a building. Inside were people, human beings such as he had been. For a moment, he had the illusion that he could see them through the walls. But no. He was seeing blue images of the people inside, much like the military's infrared devices displayed red heat signatures. He didn't understand why these were blue, though.

"*The water,*" Nilista said.

Human bodies, Winslow suddenly remembered, were composed mostly of water. Sixty-five percent, on average, he seemed to recall.

"*We call your former kind Blue Worlders, do we not?*" Nilista said.

And here Winslow had thought it was because the Earth appeared blue to the Martians through their telescopes. But the Martians could actually 'see' the water in a human body. That it appeared blue and not red baffled him, since most of the water was in the human bloodstream.

"*Be ready to gather even though we are well back,*" Nilista said.

Winslow figured she meant they were in the middle of the swarm, and those in front would make first contact.

A window was smashed to pieces, and the Gryghr poured inside. The people weren't armed. There were only five of them. A man raised a chair to strike a blow, and was immediately buried in Gryghr. The others fled, screaming hysterically.

Winslow wasn't able to gather a head but he saw it done, saw several Martians hold a struggling woman down while another took hold of her head with its grippers and tore her head off. Instantly, that particular Martian made for the nearest tunnel, about half a block away. The Martians who had been holding the woman down proceeded to rip off her arms and legs and placed them on either side of her torso.

Winslow felt a pulse of pleasure ripple through the Unity. A new head would result in a new conversion, as the Martians had done with him. And a new conversion was always cause to rejoice. An ignorant, benighted sentient from off-world would soon know the exquisite joy and fullness of the Unity.

With the humans in the building disposed of, the swarm was on the move again. Flowing back out into the street, the Gryghr headed for a towering structure further down.

Winslow recognized it as the Broadcast Center, the hub of the colony's audio and visual network. Disable them, and the Martians would severely cripple the humans' ability to resist.

Suddenly, the Gryghr in front of him slowed. The ground under him rumbled slightly, and he felt an agitation in the communal consciousness. He raised his eye stalks as high as they would extend, and was spiked by fear.

A tank had come out of a side street and swung to confront them, placing itself between the swarm and the Broadcast Center.

Winslow tried to project a warning into the Unity, to let the Gryghr know that the vehicle they faced was designed for one purpose and one purpose only: destruction. But his thought was lost amid the many.

The Gryghr at the front of the swarm raised their grippers and rushed the tank---and were incinerated in their tracks.

Winslow saw a blue image rise up into the turret on top of the tank and again tried to warn the Martians.

The loud hum of a MASER filled the night, and the foremost ranks of Gryghr broke into violent convulsions, their legs and forelimbs and eye stalks thrashing spasmodically. The convulsions didn't last long.

The remaining Gryghr scattered.

Winslow joined a prong that veered to a two-story building. They scrambled to the roof, and only then did he realize Nilista wasn't with him. She had gone the other way, to a building across the street. He could feel her but not as strongly. "*Nilista,*" he said.

"*I am here, bindmate.*"

"*What do we do?*"

"*We stay where we are. A Hryghr is coming.*"

The tank was slowly advancing. A wounded Gryghr tried to scramble out of its way, only to be riddled by twin machineguns.

A stir of resentment rippled through the Unity. Until his transformation, it had never occurred to Winslow that the Martians might have the same---or similar---emotions as humans. He'd regarded them as cold-blooded monstrosities, incapable of feeling.

The tank stopped and the soldier manning the MASER trained it on the roofs to one side and then the other.

Winslow and every other Gryghr on the roof with him dropped low, except for their eye stalks. Peering over the rim, he glimpsed gouts of fire throughout the colony, and a building that had partially collapsed. The gathering wasn't going as smoothly as the Martians hoped. By the sound and sight of things, the colonists were resisting to their utmost.

Stupid Blue Worlders, Winslow thought, and inwardly laughed at the irony. Here he was, a former Blue Worlder, criticizing those who had yet to undergo the change. They wouldn't fight back if they had any inkling of the gift the Martians wanted to bestow. It would never occur to them that the Martians might have their best interests at heart. It had never occurred to him. Who would have imagined the Martians held the secret to life eternal, or close to it?

A stir among the Gryghr heralded the arrival of a Hryghr.

Winslow edged to the roof's rim and saw the gigantic blue warrior bearing down the street directly toward the tank. That was the thing about Hryghr: They threw themselves into combat with a primal joy.

The tank had stopped and the turret gunner was yelling to the driver.

The Hryghr moved faster.

CHAPTER 27

Archard and his party covered two blocks without incident. From all quarters rose scattered screams and death wails, while furtive movements in the shadows, and skittering sounds from all over, never ceased.

Archard was grateful his small group wasn't attacked a second time. He suspected that the Martians were busy hitting specific targets, and would pick off everyone else once the colony was under their sway.

He stayed keyed to the U.N.I.C. channel and overheard an exchange between Major Howard and Private Heinlein. The latter, along with a Private Bova, were in a tank sent to defend the Broadcast Center. Apparently, the privates had engaged the Martians and routed them, and the major congratulated them on a job well done.

"Let them try again and we'll burn the bastards, sir," Private Heinlein crowed. "They go down easy."

Archard couldn't let that pass. "This is Captain Rahn, Private," he broke in. "Don't get cocky. I've fought these things. They're not pushovers."

"We can take them, sir," Private Heinlein declared.

"I like your attitude, Private," Major Howard said. "Keep pouring it on them. And Captain Archard? Unless you have something positive to contribute, maintain radio silence."

With an effort, Archard swallowed his anger.

"What's the matter? You look mad?"

Archard hadn't realized that Katla had come up, Piotr glued to her leg.

"Archard?"

"When we reach the Security Center, I'm taking you and Trisna to a bunker on the bottom level," Archard informed her. All the Security Centers had them. "It's where emergency supplies are stored. You'll be as safe there as anywhere."

"Nowhere is safe, and you know it," Katla said.

"If you keep quiet and stay still, they might not know you're there. If I can, I'll come back for you."

"You think the colony will fall, don't you?"

"There's no predicting," Archard hedged.

They hastened on, neither saying a word, until

Katla said quietly, "I hated being separated. I missed you. Worried about you."

"Same with me," Archard acknowledged.

"Where are we, Archard?" Katla said. "I don't mean here," and she gestured at the buildings and the street, "but in here." She touched her chest. "Have we taken it to the next level? In New Meridian, we dated and had feelings. But this is more, isn't it?"

"Now's not the time," Archard said.

"Then when?" Katla said. "Our lives could end around the next block." She squeezed his arm. "I'd just like to know where I stand. Am I making more of it than there is or do you feel about me the way I feel about you?"

"If we make it out of this, I'd like to go on seeing you," Archard said. "Does that answer your question?"

Katla smiled. "More or less."

"Captain!" Private Pasco said. "Everett is signaling!"

Archard had let himself be distracted. Up ahead, the Kentuckian had raised his fist in the air, the sign to freeze. Pasco, Corporal Arnold, and Private Niven already had.

"Stand still, ladies," Archard said, and glided to join Everett, who was pointing his ICW up a side street.

Martians were scurrying out of a building. One held a severed head aloft. It scurried away, and the rest, twenty or so, turned toward the intersection where Archard and Everett stood.

"Hell," Everett said.

Quickly, Archard raised his arm and moved it in a circle, the signal for Corporal Arnold and the others to close-up. They came on the run, the ladies between them.

The creatures had momentarily stopped.

"Form a skirmish line," Archard said. "Everett and I will fire incendiaries at thirty meters. Any that make it through, the rest of you take down."

"Yes, sir," Corporal Arnold said.

The next moment, the Martians hurtled forward, their eye stalks waving and dipping.

"Forty-five meters. Forty. Thirty-five. Thirty," Archard ticked off the range while angling his ICW. "Now!"

The two incendiaries left their tubes with a loud whoosh.

Splashes of fire engulfed fully half the creatures. They died writhing and flailing. The remainder came on undeterred.

Private Pasco, Corporal Arnold, and Private Niven opened up. In the space of seconds, all but one creature was down. The last put on a burst of speed, its grippers reaching for Private Everett.

Archard and the Kentuckian turned its carapace into Swiss cheese.

"Head out," Archard immediately directed. "Double time." Jogging the rest of the way would tire them, but the sooner he got the women and kids off the street, the better.

Except for the slap of their feet and their heavy breathing, they put another block behind them in silence.

Private Pasco broke it by pointing straight up and exclaiming, "Sir! What are those?"

Above the dome, something moved. A great many somethings. They flitted and darted and performed aerial circles. Now and again, one would try to alight on the dome but couldn't find purchase. The nanosheath was as sheer as glass and as slippery as ice.

"Flyers," Archard said. A new tactic on the Martians' part. They hadn't used flyers at New Meridian.

"What are they doing, sir?" Pasco said.

"Your guess is as good as mine."

"Can they breach the dome?" Katla asked.

"Let's hope not," Archard said. The explosive decompression would be devastating.

Soon, they came upon two bodies lying in the street, a man and a woman missing their heads, their arms, and legs arranged as they always were.

"Damn weird," Corporal Arnold muttered.

Out of nowhere swelled the sound of thrusters, and a RAM 3000 flew in over them, and hovered. Lieutenant Burroughs tilted the battle suit's oversized helmet to smile down at Archard, and raised the suit's huge right fist in a thumbs up. "I'm on my way to the other dome. Buzz me when you're airborne."

"Will do," Archard promised.

She rocketed away, a human-shaped metallic meteor of Promethean proportions.

"Give those ugly things hell, Lieutenant!" Corporal

Arnold shouted after her. He chuckled at Archard. "You, too, sir, when you get up there."

"I intend to," Archard said.

Kralun the Martian---Winslow was getting the hang of thinking of himself that way---stared down in fascination as the Hryghr charged the tank. The blue warriors were fierce and implacable, and Kralun felt a surge of pride that such a sentient was a brother in the Unity.

The tank opened up with its machine guns. Slugs peppered the ground in a direct line toward the Hryghr and then struck the warrior's carapace. Unlike Kralun's carapace, which wasn't thick enough to withstand small-arms fire, the Hryghr's was so hard and thick that most of the rounds either ricocheted off or barely penetrated.

The tank operator realized his machine guns weren't having much of an effect and switched to his flamethrower. A gout of flame burst toward the warrior, and the Hryghr slowed. The heat was so intense, nothing could long withstand it. Swerving clear, the warrior kept coming.

The tank operator switched to his ion cannon.

A tremendous explosion blew the Hryghr onto his side. Instantly surging erect, the warrior narrowly evaded a second cannon shell.

Kralun worried that the Hryghr would be struck head-on by the next round. But the warrior was no fool. Abruptly speeding toward a house module, it plowed through the front door as if it were so much paper, and disappeared inside.

The tank's motor revved and the tank turned to face the house. In quick succession, it fired three cannon rounds, obliterating the front of the structure.

Kralun thought the same thing that the tank operator must have thought, that he had killed the blue warrior, because the tank stopped firing.

Quivering in anticipation, Kralun waited to observe the outcome. So much dust was in the air around the house that he couldn't see a thing.

The soldiers in the tank gave voice to cries of victory.

Kralun felt a stir in the Unity, as if every Gryghr who had witnessed the battle was preparing to rush the tank in retaliation.

"Stay still," Nilista's sentience told him. *"It is not over."*

How did she know? Kralun wondered.

The tank's operator was swinging the tank around to cover the street.

Out of the building next to the demolished house hurtled the blue warrior. The Hryghr had crashed through an inner wall to escape the cannon, and was renewing its attack.

There was a startled yell from the tank. The turret swiveled and the MASER went into action.

Worry gripped Kralun. As he well knew from his former life, a MASER could kill anything. It ruptured every organ, every blood vessel.

The blue warrior darted left and then right, but the turret gunner kept the MASER on him. There was still too much ground to cover before the warrior could reach the humans.

The Hryghr suddenly changed direction, streaking toward an office building. Smashing through a window, the warrior once again disappeared.

The trooper in the turret cursed.

Kralun felt a sense of unease among the onlooking Gryghr. The attack on the golden eggs wasn't going as smoothly as they had hoped. The change in tactics to reduce casualties wasn't working. Already scores had perished. The Blue Worlders were more tenacious and resourceful than their leaders accounted for.

Once, Kralun would have been proud at how bravely and well the Earthers fought. Now, he felt only dismay that the gathering would take longer to complete, and cost many more Martian lives.

Nilista must have felt his sadness because she said, *"You become one of us more and more, bindmate."*

"*If these Blue Worlders only knew the happiness we offer them,*" Kralun lamented.

"*They are not of the Unity, as we are. They do not experience the Source of All, as we do.*"

"*Nor can they, as they are.*"

"*We came to the same conclusion after our scientists dissected and studied their bodies. Their biological organisms are quite primitive. Only the most basic of functions.*"

"*And they are fragile compared to us,*" Kralun noted.

"*Very much so, yes. If not for their machines and their weapons, we would gather and convert them without hindrance. Their technology in that respect is superior to ours.*"

"*But that's the thing,*" Kralun said. "*Our biology is superior to their technology. In the end, we will prevail.*"

"*Listen to you,*" Nilista said, her sentience laced with amusement. "*Praising us over them.*"

Down below, the tank operator had turned the vehicle so it covered the building the warrior had gone into.

Kralun was pleasantly taken aback when the Hryghr burst out of a building behind the tank, on the other side of the street. The explanation, Kralun realized, was that there must be a tunnel under it, either dug by the drillers or a maintenance tunnel.

The turret gunner heard the crash of glass and the splintering of the module, and with his three hundred and sixty-degree field of view, whipped his head around and saw the warrior. He yelled to the tank operator even as he began to turn the turret. As quick as he was, though, he wasn't quick enough.

The Hryghr rammed into the rear of the tank like a rhino into a rival. The impact lifted the tank off its wheels and it nearly went over. Only its weight saved it. Slamming back down, the tank was now broadside to the Hryghr. The warrior smashed into it, causing the turret gunner to grab for support.

The tank's operator threw the tank into reverse. Tires squealing, it sped back a good twenty meters and braked to a stop with its front end again pointed at the warrior. Its machine guns cut loose, the flame thrower belched fire.

The Hryghr threw itself at its mechanical foe. Carapace lowered, it withstood the withering lead-and-fire storm.

If Kralun still had human vocal chords, he would have cheered.

The blue warrior's iron-hard grippers shattered the tank's windshield. The operator yelled and must have tromped on the gas because the tank's wheels spun furiously. Only this time, the warrior had hold, down near the undercarriage, and through sheer strength, held the tank in place.

The turret gunner popped the turret and leaned out, an ICW to his shoulder. He fired at the Hryghr's broad back, his rounds having no more effect than a pea shooter on a turtle shell.

With a prodigious effort, the blue warrior tore the front of the tank open. Like an antique can opener opening a can, the warrior peeled the alloy apart wide enough for it to suddenly lunge and seize the driver. The man screamed as the warrior's grippers sheared through his uniform. Flesh and bone were reduced to pulp.

Scrambling out of the turret, the gunner sprang to the back of the tank, jumped down, and raced pell-mell toward the Broadcast Center.

An impulse swept the Unity. As one, Kralun and the other Gryghr scrambled from the buildings, and gave chase. His thoughts were the same as his new kindred's.

The Blue Worlders would be converted whether they liked it or not.

CHAPTER 28

Climbing into the battered and dented RAM 3000 was like reuniting with an old friend. Archard gave the open chest plate an affectionate pat, scaled the last couple of rungs on the massive frame that held the battle suit at the ready, and eased into the gigantic exoskeleton.

The Robotic Armored Man-of-War was first used in combat on Earth decades ago. Since then, it had undergone continuous modification and improvement. When it was announced that the United Nations had decided to send a RAM to each of the colonies on Mars, the decision was met with widespread derision. What use was there for the ultimate fighting machine on a planet where there was no one to fight?

The public didn't know what the powers-that-be knew. That Mars was inhabited, and the things that inhabited it might take exception to the intruders from another world.

Archard nodded down at Private Everett, who was at a console below, and Everett began releasing the clamps on the frame.

Private Pasco was over by a dolly he had used to wheel in magnetic bombs and flamethrower canisters. "You are locked and loaded, sir."

"Thank you, Private." Sliding his arms into the suit's arms, Archard pressed an inner stud in the huge left hand to close the massive chest plate. He pressed another to lower the helmet and seal it. Fully encased, he activated the helmet's holo display and initiated a systems diagnostic.

Over by a wall, Katla stood watching. She was wringing her hands, her lovely face a mirror of worry.

Their arrival at the Security Center had been uneventful.

No one was there. Lieutenant Burroughs was off in the other RAM 3000. Major Howard and Sergeant Kline were out in a tank, Privates Bova and Heinlein in another.

Corporal Arnold and Private Niven had wasted no time in firing up the third and gone off into the shadowed streets to aid in the colony's defense.

"Private Everett, Private Pasco," Archard said through his speakers. "Once I'm outside, secure the ramp door. It's your job to protect Dr. Dkany and Ms. Sahir while I'm gone."

"But sir," Pasco said, "shouldn't we be out in the streets with the rest of you?"

"Someone should be at headquarters," Archard said. "Consider yourselves our reserves in case the worst comes to pass."

"And if it does, sir?" Private Everett said.

"Abandon the colony."

"Not again," Private Pasco said.

"You can't fight the Martians alone," Archard said. "There are other rovers besides the tanks. Take one, and the ladies and the kids, and do what you can to stay alive long enough to be rescued."

"By who?" Private Everett said. "Do the bigwigs at Bradbury know we're under attack?"

Archard hadn't thought to ask Chief Administrator Reubens if he had contacted the governor. Even if Reubens had, it could well be another blackout had been imposed to prevent the colonists at Bradbury from learning about the Martians. Archard wouldn't put anything past their so-called leaders. "I have no idea," he admitted.

"Different planet, same FUBARs," Everett said.

The last of the clamps disengaged. Archard took a couple of steps away from the frame, the battle suit's enormous boots coming down with ponderous thuds. He raised and lowered the RAM's arms a few times, testing. Everything appeared to be functioning as it should, an assessment confirmed by the diagnostic. He thought to check the internal maintenance log and discovered that Lieutenant Burroughs had been working on repairs before the Martians attacked. The RAM 3000 was good to go.

"Open the ramp door," Archard commanded. As it rose, he turned and smiled at Katla. "I expect to be gone a while. Stay safe."

"You too," Katla said, and swallowed.

Archard tried to lighten her mood. "I have help this time. Burroughs is in the other RAM, and there are three tanks, not just one."

"Will it be enough?"

"Cup always full, remember?" Archard said.

Katla smiled, albeit half-heartedly. "Yes. That's you to a T. You never give up."

"Booyah," Archard said, and was immediately echoed by Everett and Pasco. Clomping up the ramp, Archard monitored the suit's gyros to ensure the stabilizers were working as they should. He had worn the battle suit for so long on the thousand-kilometer-plus trek from New Meridian to Wellsville that it seemed more like a second skin than a machine.

Archard strode into the open. The light from his helmet and his chest plate lit up his surroundings brighter than day. He switched on his spotlight and swept the area for a hundred meters around.

No Martians.

"Close the ramp door," Archard said. Only when it thunked shut did he kick in the thrusters and go airborne.

Ascending in a wide spiral, Archard rose until he was only a dozen meters below the dome. Amplifying the RAM's input feeds, he was immersed in a visual and audio spectacle of utter bedlam.

Martians were everywhere. Damaged structures showed jagged holes. Debris littered many of the streets. So did more than a few bodies. A shriek pierced the night, and in the vicinity of the Administrative Center a tank cannon boomed.

None of the fires that had started when the Martians burst into buildings and disrupted the electrical systems had lasted long. The building modules weren't flammable, and the contents that had been set ablaze were extinguished by the sprinklers. Which was why smoke was rising from various quarters, a cloud of it covering an entire block.

Archard spied a cluster of creatures moving along a side street in the general direction of the Security Center. Banking, he flew to the near end of the street, zoomed in on the Martians with the RAM's night vision, and set his targeting system on automatic. Tiny crosshairs appeared on each image. All he had to do was select the weapon to be used. Archard chose a dart. It flew true and was almost to the Martians when it separated into its one hundred component flechettes. Every Martian was struck by multiple razors and died oozing the viscous fluid that passed for their blood.

"Security Center, do you read me?" Archard said.

"Loud and clear, sir," Private Everett responded.

"Be advised, I just took out a gaggle of Martians in your vicinity."

"A gaggle, sir?"

"Be on the lookout for more."

"Will do, sir."

Archard regained altitude. His motion sensors pinged, reacting to the presence of the flyers above the dome. He was about to go investigate a column of smoke near the Broadcast Center when his commlink blared.

"Captain Rahn! This is Lieutenant Burroughs. Do you copy?" Her tone suggested a crisis.

"Rahn here," Archard quickly answered.

"I'm in Dome One. I require your assistance ASAP."

"I can be there in five," Archard said.

"Make it sooner."

As he boosted his thrusters, Archard said, "Where are you exactly, and what is your situation?"

"I'm at the hospital," she replied, "and we're being overrun."

Dome One and Dome Two were linked by a modular walkway wide enough for a tank and high enough that when Archard reached it, he only needed to bend at the RAM's knees to make it through.

As he emerged, Archard heard a chorus of terrified screams and panicked cries, along with the unmistakable sounds of a pitched battle. One look, and an oath escaped him.

Dome One was suffering the brunt of the Martian onslaught. Twice the number of structures were damaged, and many times the number of bodies lay in the streets. The hospital, situated at the center, was the tallest building. Smoke curled from several stories.

Archard took it all in as he took to the air once more. Pegging the thrusters, he swept in over the hospital.

Hundreds upon hundreds of Martians were pouring up out of newly made tunnels and sweeping out of side streets to converge en masse on the colony's facility for treating the sick. And there, close to the hospital, was Lieutenant Burroughs in the other RAM 3000, single-handedly resisting the onslaught. She unleashed a missile, incinerated onrushing creatures with her flamethrower, and used her Minigun. Arcing up and over the roof, she blasted Martians attacking from the rear.

"Not on my watch!" Archard heard her shout. "Not on my watch!"

His thrusters roaring, Archard descended to her side. "The cavalry has arrived. Do you want the front or the back?"

"The back is fine," Burroughs said, and flashed him a smile through her faceplate. "And thank you."

"Kick ass," Archard said. Propelling to the front, he suited his actions to his command and opened up with his ion cannons. Martians were destroyed in droves. He lobbed bombs to either side of the hospital, their detonators set to go off on impact.

Dropping to block the entrance, Archard loosed three frag grenades in rapid succession. They landed so close together that they not only reduced dozens of creatures to blasted pieces, they created a small crater.

And still the Martians came.

To Archard, it was his battle under Albor Tholus all over again. Only this time, he didn't have to contend with the flyers. And, so far, he hadn't seen any of the blue S.O.B.'s that were so hard to kill.

His commlink chirped, Lieutenant Burroughs exclaiming, "They're coming in waves!"

"Same here!" Archard told her.

He slaughtered with ruthless abandon. That he was protecting helpless patients had something to do with it. So did the fact he had grown to despise the Martians with a deep and bitter hatred. They never showed mercy, never any compassion. They were all about killing. They ripped people apart with no more regard than if humans were vermin to be exterminated. He could not slay the creatures fast enough.

For their part, the Martians assaulting the hospital displayed the tenacity typical of their kind. Archard mowed them down, and still they attacked. He blistered them, he incinerated them, and still they charged. His darts sliced them to pieces, his missiles blew them to atoms, and still they sought to get past him.

Archard used every weapon in the RAM's arsenal. And just when he began to wonder if it would be enough, if he would, in fact, run out of ammo before he ran out of creatures to kill, the waves lessened and finally, ultimately, stopped entirely.

Suspecting a ruse, Archard hovered and took stock. He had one Penetrator missile left, four darts, and half a dozen grenades. His ion cannons were recharging, but he was out of magnetic bombs. The flame thrower was running low. And he only had about two thousand rounds left for the M537 Minigun.

A sound caused Archard to turn and raise his right gauntlet, but he didn't fire. "All clear back there?"

"They've stopped for the moment," Lieutenant Burroughs said, descending. "Thank God. I'm almost on empty on everything."

"Head for the Security Center and rearm," Archard said. "Private Everett and Private Pasco will help. They know the drill. I'll hold the fort here."

"Maybe we should stick together, sir."

Archard was about to tell her it was an order, not a request, when a low rumbling filled his earpieces and up the street chugged a tank. Dents and scratches showed it had been in the heat of combat.

"Captain Rahn, sir!"

"Corporal Arnold?" Archard had almost forgotten that Major Howard sent the corporal to defend Dome One.

"And Private Niven, sir," Arnold said. "We had a firefight with those things or we'd have been here sooner."

"How low are you on shells and ammo?"

"Plenty left," Corporal Arnold said.

Archard opted to take a gamble. "I want you to stay here and defend the hospital while Lieutenant Burroughs and I head to the Security Center. We're about dry." In his estimation, it was worth the risk if it meant having both battle suits at peak performance. "We'll refit and hurry back."

"Take your time, sir," Corporal Arnold said. "From the sound of things, the Martians have called it quits."

Archard boosted the gain on his helmet audio input---and realized Dome One had gone quiet. The screaming had stopped. So had the scuttling sounds of the creatures.

"They might be reassembling to try again," Lieutenant Burroughs said.

"Or maybe they're going after the other dome, sir," Corporal Arnold said.

Archard hadn't thought of that. It made tactical sense, though. If the Martians were more hard-pressed in one dome than the other, they might concentrate their forces on the weaker. Once it fell, they could throw everything at the hardest to take.

"On me, Lieutenant," Archard said, and rose higher. "Corporal, we leave the hospital in your hands until we get back."

"No worries, sir," Arnold said.

"At full thrust, Lieutenant, on my mark," Archard said. "Now!"

Together, they arced toward the walkway, twin humanoid rockets blazing in the artificial atmosphere of the golden dome.

Archard was impressed by how Burroughs handled her RAM. She matched his every more. When he slowed to descend, she was his shadow. Their heavy boots thudded to the ground, and Burroughs fell into step beside him.

Archard tried his commlink. "Major Howard, can you read me?" He was overdue for a sitrep on the other dome.

There was no answer.

"Let me try, sir," Lieutenant Burroughs said, and repeated his call.

Again, no reply.

"Not good," Archard said.

"Could be interference of some kind," Burroughs said.

"This close?" Archard said skeptically. Only long-range communications were affected by a blackout. Local channels still got through. "Sergeant Kline? Private Heinlein? Private Bova? Do any of you read me?"

Static hissed like bacon in a frying pan.

"It can't be," Burroughs said. "Not all of them. We'd have heard something."

"We'll find out soon enough," Archard said grimly, and hurried on.

CHAPTER 29

Kralun the Martian raced along a tunnel with hundreds of his fellow Gryghr, Nilista once again at his side. Even though they had only been separated a short while, reuniting with her had made him deliriously happy. She had sensed his feeling, and explained that bindmates joined in more than bodies. They were bound to one another in their very sentience.

In his former life as a Blue Worlder, Kralun would never have imagined crustaceans capable of such depth of emotion. But then, there was a lot about the Martians he would never have imagined.

His main concern at the moment, though, was their attack on the golden eggs. It wasn't going well. The initial plan to overwhelm the Blue Worlders by force of numbers with minimal loss of Unity life had not worked out.

Kralun blamed their failure on several factors. For one thing, there were a lot more humans at Wellsville than there had been at New Meridian. Gathering them took longer. That delay gave the human military time to respond. And there were a lot more soldiers, with a lot more weapons.

It didn't bother Kralun that the Aryghr and Hryghr had miscalculated. Martians weren't perfect. They were no different than Blue Worlders when it came to making mistakes.

And their miscalculations were now being remedied.

Reinforcements were pouring in from all over. In the meantime, those already there were to use the new tunnels the drillers were burrowing to attack select targets.

Which was what Kralun and those with him were about to do. A tank was protecting the Administrative Center, and the Hryghr were marshaling a great number of Gryghr to assist in taking it out.

Kralun realized he was still thinking mostly in Blue World terms, and chided himself.

Nilista, aware of his every thought, sought to comfort him with, *"What you are going through is normal, bindmate. The transformation does not take place in a single night. It is a continuous process. In the fullness of time, you will fully be one of us. Never fear."*

"With you at my side, I don't."

"You should merge with the Unity again, bindmate," Nilista said. *"There is much being imparted."*

It was harder for him than it was for her because he was so new at it. It also left him feeling drained. But he did as she wanted and felt himself immersed in the river of collective consciousness. Without having to sort and sift, he became aware of certain aspects of the attack.

Their leaders estimated that about half the Blue Worlders had been gathered so far, their heads en route to the laboratories of the Eryghr.

Kralun also learned that the assault on the golden egg that harbored the hospital had not gone well. An army of Gryghr had been repulsed by a pair of RAM 3000's.

The Martians didn't call them that, of course. To the natives, the battle suits were regarded much as they regarded their own carapaces, as hard shells that shielded their internal organs. And that was what they called the RAM's: Hard Shells. Of all the human weapons, the Martians were most wary of those.

Kralun reminded himself that he had to stop thinking of the Martians 'as' Martians. They were not any such thing. They were the Unity.

"We near the hive that rules," Nilista said.

Kralun slipped out of the communal awareness to be himself again. He couldn't do both at the same time, as Nilista could. That would take a lot of practice.

The tunnel brought them up into a large dark building where the Gryghr were massing, only a block from the Administrative Center.

Kralun could see it off through the front window. He could also see the tank positioned in front of it.

"Any moment," Nilista said.

No sooner did she tell him than a Hryghr crashed out of a building further down, close to the tank. Like a living battering ram, the blue warrior hurtled to the attack. Kralun expected a repeat of what he had witnessed earlier. The warrior would prevail, the tank would be destroyed.

But the Hryghr was not even halfway to its nemesis when the ground under it erupted in a titanic explosion.

The Hryghr, as huge and heavy as it was, was flung into the air and literally ripped in half.

A mine! Kralun realized. The humans had mined the approaches to the Admin Center.

The blue warrior was dead before its parts hit the ground.

As if they were endowed with but one mind and one purpose, the Gryghr poured out into the street to avenge him.

Kralun tried to warn them. He tried to insert himself into the Unity and project images of mines, but he was too inexperienced.

Those out in front were reduced to fragments by a second blast. Those behind them pressed on and met their end by yet another, pieces cascading down like so many hailstones.

Thankfully, Kralun was well back in the swarm. But he was far from out of danger. The tank's operator had opened up with its ion cannon, to devastating effect. A dozen Gryghr near him were reduced to their elements in midstride.

The turret gunner was doing his part, too. Martian after Martian fell as the MASER turned their insides to jelly.

The attack wasn't going well. Were Kralun in charge, he would call it off to regroup. But the Gryghr showed no inclination to retreat. Those slain were instantly replaced by those coming after them. Hundreds died. Hundreds more would have, except that, to Kralun's surprise and joy, a hole suddenly appeared under the tank. A driller had come up from below. The hole rapidly widened, and the driller withdrew. Drillers weren't fighters.

The tank's rear tilted down. The operator reacted by throwing the tank into drive, its tires seeking purchase that wasn't there. Kralun recognized the gleam of insignia on the driver's suit. It was an officer. A major.

With no traction so it could right itself, the tank became stuck in the hole. Its front end was pointed at the dome, effectually rendering much of its armament useless.

The turret gunner made it out and ran for the Admin entrance, ducking inside.

The major left his seat and scrambled to the turret, but he wasn't quite out when the foremost Gryghr reached him. In the heat of combat, with the loss of so many of their fellows a gaping hurt in the Unity, they forgot their purpose. Instead of ripping off the major's head and taking it back to convert, they tore him into particles no bigger than a human fingernail.

Kralun got there in time to join in. His grippers fastened on a booted foot, which he gleefully tore off.

In the flush of victory, the Gryghr raised their grippers to the stars.

Suddenly, Kralun became aware of a stir of apprehension. He turned his eye stalks in the direction the rest were turning, and shared in their unease. Down the block new enemies hovered.

A pair of Hard Shells.

Captain Archard Rahn and Lieutenant Ula Burroughs took longer than Archard liked to rearm their battle suits. Even with Everett and Pasco helping, the ammunition, darts, missiles, and grenades had to be wheeled down the short hall from the armory, then carefully raised by a mechanical arm and just as carefully loaded. Although trained to prep a battle suit in under ten minutes, it took almost half an hour before both RAM's were ready to reengage the enemy.

Katla and Trisna and the children watched, prudently staying out of the way. It was obvious to Archard that Katla wanted him to go over and talk to her, but he didn't have the time. He needed to get back to Dome One, and the hospital. To that end, as soon as the suits were ready, he waved to her and sealed himself in.

Archard was first up the ramp and the first to go airborne. They started toward the other dome just as their commlinks blared.

"Mayday! Mayday! To all U.N.I.C. personnel! This is Major Howard! Sergeant Kline and I need immediate assistance at Admin! Repeat! Immediate assistance is required! All units respond!"

Archard keyed his mic. "This is Captain Rahn. Lieutenant Burroughs and I are on our way." He swooped toward the Administrative Center.

Burroughs, doing her shadowing act, said, "What about the hospital?"

"This shouldn't take long," Archard hoped. That they were late getting back to Corporal Arnold was bothering him, too.

Thrusters at full, they soared over damaged buildings and debris and scattered torsos and arms and legs. In vain, Archard sought for the heat signatures of colonists still alive. The Administrative Center came into view, and the street in front of it.

"Dear God," Burroughs breathed.

Archard brought his RAM to a stop and once again hovered. The area around Admin literally crawled with creatures. The tank had fallen into a hole and was being ripped apart. So was a trooper. Magnifying the visual feed, he recognized the face frozen in a death cry.

"Major Howard!" Burroughs gasped.

"I don't see Sergeant Kline," Archard said. He hoped the noncom had made it inside. He counted seven heat signatures, all on the top floor except one that was rising in an elevator.

"The creatures see us, sir," Burroughs said.

As one, the Martians had turned and raised their eerie eyes. As one, their grippers rose in what might be construed as a gesture of defiance.

"Do we engage?" Lieutenant Burroughs asked.

"We sure as hell do."

Kralun of the Unity would gladly have waited for a Hryghr to arrive but his fellow Gryghr didn't share his caution. The

They didn't appreciate the sheer lethality of the battle suits.

"*Stay close to me, bindmate,*" Nilista said.

"*Always,*" Kralun said, although secretly he would rather flee. He should have remembered that she could feel his every thought.

"*Do not despair. We are the Unity. We are strong. We will prevail.*"

"*There are two Hard Shells,*" Kralun said.

"*And we are many. With more on the way.*"

Kralun was heartened to see Gryghr suddenly flow out of side streets and over nearby rooftops to join in the impending fray.

"*Do you see, bindmate?*" Nilista said. "*We are never alone in the Unity. In our numbers is our strength. We serve the Source of All, and cannot fail.*"

Kralun didn't share her deeply spiritual nature. It was something to discuss another day.

The Hard Shells were on the move. Side-by-side, they slowly advanced. When they extended their huge right arms, Kralun thought they were going to fire missiles or darts or grenades. But no. Narrow beams of brilliant red light shot from their wrist gauntlets, slicing through everything the beams touched.

Lasers! Kralun realized. No one had ever told him the U.N.I.C. brought lasers to Mars. He yearned more than ever to get out of there but he was hemmed by his fellow Gryghr. He must do as they were doing. He must attack.

Earlier, at the Security Center, Archard had been loading grenades into his RAM when Private Everett hurried in from the armory with a big grin on his face. The Kentuckian was holding something behind his back.

"I thought I saw them and I wasn't sure so I went to double check," Everett said. "You're going to be plumb giddy, sir."

Without stopping his work, Archard said, "I could use some giddiness right about now."

Everett brought his hands out. In the palm of each was a compact rectangular unit with what appeared to be the nozzle of a spray gun protruding fifteen centimeters from an end.

"What…?" Archard said.

Everett turned one of the units over. The bottom was slotted in the same fashion as the dart and missile units that Archard had just got done attaching to the RAM's wrist gauntlets.

"They're for the RAM?" Archard said, trying to remember where he might have seen similar units before.

Chuckling, Private Everett held the side of one of the units up so Archard could see the serial number and the model type imprinted in red ink.

"Laser," Archard read in amazement.

"Two of them, sir," Private Everett said. "One for each of you."

Quickly, Archard descended to examine one. Lasers were ridiculously expensive to manufacture, and were notorious for using too much power. But they were the crème de la crème of U.N.I.C. armaments, the deadliest weapon in their arsenal. And that was saying a lot. "I didn't know there were any on Mars."

"Do you want them fitted on the suits?" Private Everett said.

"Do you even need to ask?" Archard retorted.

It delayed the rearming but it was worth it. Now, with Burroughs at his side, Archard flew to within a hundred meters of the creatures milling around the tank and extended his arm. A good thing he did, because out of the side streets and over the rooftops flowed more Martians.

"Let them have it, Lieutenant," Archard said. "Lasers, if you please."

"With pleasure, sir," Burroughs said.

Archard fired. There was a soft hiss, like air escaping from a tire, and a bright red beam shot from the nozzle on his wrist. The effect was spectacular. He and Burroughs cut the creatures into halves and thirds and spilled their insides. Martian after Martian after Martian. It didn't matter how fast the things moved, they couldn't outrun the speed of light. Methodically sweeping the beams back and forth, he and Burroughs slew the creatures by the hundreds.

He heard Burroughs laugh.

Kralun saw the reinforcements being laid low and tingled with an urge to destroy their slayers. That was the Martian part of him. His human self was screaming to get out of there, to run before it was too late.

"*Be strong, bindmate*," Nilista said.

On all sides, Martians scrambled toward the Hard Shells, sweeping Kralun along. He tried to merge with the Unity to warn them to get out of there, but he was too rattled to concentrate.

The Gryghr were rushing to their doom and didn't know it.

Then, around a building, came a Hryghr. At this, an inner pulse of support went up from the Gryghr, the equivalent of a resounding cheer on Earth. The blue warrior charged toward the

Hard Shells, fearless, determined. Here was the toughest of them, the mightiest of them.

One of the Hard Shells moved an arm and sliced the Hryghr down the middle.

Dismay gripped the Gryghr. To a Martian, they slowed in consternation.

Surely now, Kralun thought, they would realize the folly of their attack. They would see that the wisest recourse was to retreat.

All the Gryghr began to shake. Even Nilista. He sensed that it stemmed from their communal consciousness, and merged to find out why.

"*Brothers! Sisters!*" a Martian was saying. "*You have seen! Let us avenge those who have been lost! Let us rise up in our numbers and tear these Hard Shells apart. We can do it! We are the Unity! And in our union we are strong! Flow with me! Let us show these Blue Worlders that those who follow the Source of All are not afraid to merge with the Source should the need arise! Onward! To battle!*"

Kralun couldn't believe what he was sensing. The troops were being rallied, Martian style. "*No!*" he shouted. "*It is a mistake! This is not the way!*"

"*They cannot sense your warning, bindmate,*" Nilista said.

Once more, Kralun was swept forward by the press. He struggled to break free. He did not want to die. Not when the Martians had given him the priceless gift of a life span measured in thousands of years, if not longer. He wanted to live those thousands. To live forever, if he could. To hell with merging with the Source.

"*Oh, bindmate,*" Nilista said.

They were closing on the Hard Shells. Kralun saw the faceplate of the one on the right and recognition caused him to trip and almost fall. It was Captain Archard Rahn, his former U.N.I.C. liaison at New Meridian. Archard! he wished he could scream. Don't shoot! It's me! Levlin Winslow!

Another instant, and Winslow found himself staring directly into the laser beam. Bright red light filled his vision, his world, his universe. There was the red light and only the red light. He vaguely thought he felt Nilista, and then there was a searing season, and then nothing, nothing at all.

Archard and Lieutenant Burroughs killed and killed and killed some more. When the number of Martians dwindled, Archard switched to missiles and darts to spare the power cells in their RAM's from additional drain.

At last, at long last, the sole remaining creature lay in fragments. For the moment, at least, the dome, and everything under it, was still.

"Heat sig, sir," Burroughs said.

Archard's helmet holo showed someone descending in the elevator in the Administrative Center. The other heat signatures were no longer there. Descending to ground level, he stepped over mounds of dead creatures to reach the entrance.

Out staggered Sergeant Kline. His EVA suit was torn and he was bleeding from a leg wound, but he tiredly smiled and said, "Good to see you made it, sirs."

"What happened up there?" Archard wanted to know.

"Martians came in through the windows while you were fighting these," Kline said, nodding at the heaps. "I tried to protect Chief Administrator Reubens and those with him. There were just too many of the things. I barely made it out myself."

"Reubens is definitely dead?"

"I saw a Martian rip his head off and go running out a window with it."

"Then we won't see him again," Archard said.

"Lieutenant Burroughs, I want you to take Sergeant Kline to the Security Center. Both of you are to stay there until you hear from me."

"But sir..." Burroughs began to protest.

"It's the only way to get the sergeant there safely," Archard said. "I'll check on Corporal Arnold and the hospital and bring everyone still alive back with me."

"Yes, sir," Burroughs said reluctantly.

"You don't need to baby me, sir," Sergeant Kline said. "I can manage on my own. She can go with you."

"I'm sorry," Archard said. "When did this become a democracy? With Major Howard dead, I'm in command. You will follow orders, the both of you."

At their mutual, "Yes, sir!" Archard stepped back, activated his thrusters, and streaked toward Dome One. He hoped against hope that when he got there, he would find Arnold and Niven and the hospital staff and patients still alive.

Once through the walkway, he cleaved the air like a bullet. He tried repeatedly to raise the corporal, without success.

Then he saw why.

The tank, or what was left of it, lay on its side near the emergency doors. Corporal Arnold's torso and arms and legs were nearby, but not his head. Of Niven, there was no sign.

The hospital was completely dark, and quiet. Not a single heat signature showed. Archard resorted to the battle suit's megaphone and rose from floor to floor, calling for survivors to make their presence known. None did.

Dejected, Archard climbed higher. No sounds issued from under the dome. He didn't detect any sign of life.

Dome One had fallen. Every colonist in it had been lost.

Refusing to concede defeat, Archard returned to Dome Two and flew from end to end. It was more of the same. There was no life anywhere except for those waiting for him at U.N.I.C. headquarters.

One last time, Archard hovered and gazed out over the desolation. "Colony down," he said to himself, and would have wept if he could afford the time for tears. There were still lives to save, and by God, he was going to save them.

EPILOGUE

The decision was a no-brainer. They were the only humans left. Just the nine of them; Archard, Burroughs, Kline, Everett, Pasco, Katla, Trisna, Behula and Piotr.

"We don't stand a chance if we stay," Archard summed up his assessment in the Security Center mess shortly after he'd returned. "We might try to hold out if we knew help was coming, but we don't."

"I've tried and tried to raise Bradbury, sir," Private Pasco said. "They're not answering."

"Another blackout, damn their souls," Katla said.

"Regardless, we still have our tank from New Meridian," Archard reminded them. "Major Howard never got around to repairing it, but I think we can have it fitted to go by noon. Then all of you can pile in, and the lieutenant and I will take turns pushing it to Bradbury."

"That will take weeks," Trisna said, aghast. "Cooped up like before."

"Hold on," Lieutenant Burroughs said, lowering her legs from the table where she had propped them. "There's a faster way. It will be just as crowded, but we can get there in half a day."

"Are you fixing to pull a rocket out of your pocket, Lieutenant?" Private Everett joked.

"No," Burroughs said. "A Thunderbolt."

Looks of incredulity and hope spread from face to face.

Archard found his voice first. "You're a pilot? You can fly that thing?"

"I am and I can," Burroughs said. "I'm not the hotshot the major was. But I've taken the Bolt for a spin a few times, and I'm confident I can get us to Bradbury in one piece."

"Well, I'll be darned," Everett said, and laughed.

"Oh my," Trisna said, her hand to her throat. "We will live through this, after all." She scooped Behula up and spun in a circle.

"Do you believe this, sir?" Private Pasco happily said to Archard. "A stroke of luck for once."

"We were overdue," Archard said.

"What happens when we get there?" Katla said. "Will it be Wellsville all over again?"

"Let's hope not," Archard said. "There's only one colony left." He meant it jokingly but everyone sobered and stopped smiling.

"They better not muck with us," Sergeant Kline said. "If they try to pull the same thing at Bradbury that Reubens and the major pulled here, we'll call them on it."

"I hear that," Private Everett said.

"Listen up," Archard said loudly to get their attention. "It would be nice if we could take showers and enjoy a good meal and then have six or seven hours of sleep. But we don't know when the Martians will return. It could be tomorrow. It could be five minutes from now. So here's the drill." He paused. "Grab whatever you want to take so long as it's light and doesn't take up much space. Then we'll load the supplies we need and be out of here inside an hour. Any objections?"

"Are you kidding, sir?" Private Pasco said.

"Hop to it."

Since Archard didn't have personal belongings to take, he spent his time carting cases of water bottles and food to the hangar. He was on his third trip when Katla and Piotr showed up. She took the boy into the Thunderbolt and came back out alone.

"Have a moment?"

"Would that it were more," Archard said.

Katla placed her cheek on his chest and her hand on his shoulder. "Let me stand here a bit."

"It's getting to you, isn't it?"

"How can it not?" Katla said sadly.

"Once we reach Bradbury, everything will be fine."

Katla looked him in the eyes. "You don't really believe that, do you?"

"I don't know what to believe anymore," Archard confessed.

"I do," Katla said. "I believe in me and I believe in you. I believe in our new friends. I believe that together we can reach

Bradbury. After that, who knows? So long as you're with me, I don't much care."

Archard did something he hadn't done in many days. He kissed her.

Later, their provisions stocked and everyone either strapped in or seated where they could brace themselves, Lieutenant Burroughs eased the Thunderbolt from the hangar and took to the air.

Archard felt a profound sense of relief. For a while, they would be spared the hideous perils of the Red Planet. Once they arrived at Bradbury, Governor Blanchard would impose a state of emergency and contact Earth for help. With any luck, more troops and tanks and RAM 3000's would be sent. With any luck, the Martians wouldn't attack before the reinforcements landed.

And with any luck, in the end, Earth would win the war of the worlds.

FINI

CHECK OUT OTHER GREAT SCIENCE FICTION BOOKS

IN PERPETUITY
by Jake Bible

For two thousand years, Earth and her many colonies across the galaxy have fought against the Estelian menace. Having faced overwhelming losses, the CSC has instituted the largest military draft ever, conscripting millions into the battle against the aliens. Major Bartram North has been tasked with the unenviable task of coordinating the military education of hundreds of thousands of recruits and turning them into troops ready to fight and die for the cause.

As Major North struggles to maintain a training pace that the CSC insists upon, he realizes something isn't right on the Perpetuity. But before he can investigate, the station dissolves into madness brought on by the physical booster known as pharma. Unfortunately for Major North, that is not the only nightmare he faces- an armada of Estelian warships is on the edge of the solar system and headed right for Earth!

BATTLEFIELD MARS
by David Robbins

Several centuries into the future, Earth has established three colonies on Mars. No indigenous life has been discovered, and humankind looks forward to making the Red Planet their own.

Then 'something' emerges out of a long-extinct volcano and doesn't like what the humans are doing.

Captain Archard Rahn, United Nations Interplanetary Corps, tries to stem the rising tide of slaughter. But the Martians are more than they seem, and it isn't long before Mars erupts in all-out war.

CHECK OUT OTHER GREAT
SCIENCE FICTION BOOKS

SALVAGE MERC ONE
by Jake Bible

Joseph Laribeau was born to be a Marine in the Galactic Fleet. He was born to fight the alien enemies known as the Skrang Alliance and travel the galaxy doing his duty as a Marine Sergeant. But when the War ended and Joe found himself medically discharged, the best job ever was over and he never thought he'd find his way again.

Then a beautiful alien walked into his life and offered him a chance at something even greater than the Fleet, a chance to serve with the Salvage Merc Corp.

Now known as Salvage Merc One Eighty-Four, Joe Laribeau is given the ultimate assignment by the SMC bosses. To his surprise it is neither a military nor a corporate salvage. Rather, Joe has to risk his life for one of his own. He has to find and bring back the legend that started the Corp.

SERENGETI
by J.B. Rockwell

It was supposed to be an easy job: find the Dark Star Revolution Starships, destroy them, and go home. But a booby-trapped vessel decimates the Meridian Alliance fleet, leaving Serengeti—a Valkyrie class warship with a sentient AI brain—on her own; wrecked and abandoned in an empty expanse of space. On the edge of total failure, Serengeti thinks only of her crew. She herds the survivors into a lifeboat, intending to sling them into space. But the escape pod sticks in her belly, locking the cryogenically frozen crew inside.

Then a scavenger ship arrives to pick Serengeti's bones clean. Her engines dead, her guns long silenced, Serengeti and her last two robots must find a way to fight the scavengers off and save the crew trapped inside her.

CHECK OUT OTHER GREAT SCIENCE FICTION BOOKS

MAUSOLEUM 2069
by Rick Jones

Political dignitaries including the President of the Federation gather for a ceremony onboard Mausoleum 2069. But when a cloud of interstellar dust passes through the galaxy and eclipses Earth, the tenants within the walls of Mausoleum 2069 are reborn and the undead begin to rise. As the struggle between life and death onboard the mausoleum develops, Eriq Wyman, a one-time member of a Special ops team called the Force Elite, is given the task to lead the President to the safety of Earth. But is Earth like Mausoleum 2069? A landscape of the living dead? Has the war of the Apocalypse finally begun? With so many questions there is only one certainty: in space there is nowhere to run and nowhere to hide.

RED CARBON
by D.J. Goodman

Diamonds have been discovered on Mars.

After years of neglect to space programs around the world, a ruthless corporation has made it to the Red Planet first, establishing their own mining operation with its own rules and laws, its own class system, and little oversight from Earth. Conditions are harsh, but its people have learned how to make the Martian colony home.

But something has gone catastrophically wrong on Earth. As the colony leaders try to cover it up, hacker Leah Hartnup is getting suspicious. Her boundless curiosity will lead her to a horrifying truth: they are cut off, possibly forever. There are no more supplies coming. There will be no more support. There is no more mission to accomplish. All that's left is one goal: survival.

Printed in Poland
by Amazon Fulfillment
Poland Sp. z o.o., Wrocław